Folk Tales   398

WINGED MAGIC

'Barbara Sleigh knows how to capture
the young imagination and John
Patience completes this bit of magic
with some very fine illustrations.'
The Oxford Times

This international selection of folk tales
about flying creatures results in an
unusual and varied anthology. Children
will love the simple re-tellings, and the
stories lend themselves to being read
aloud.

About the author

Barbara Sleigh started her career as a
teacher before joining the staff of BBC
Children's Hour. She went on to write
many books for children, and in
addition, an autobiography. She loved
all her young readers, and personally
answered her letters from them up until
her death early in 1982.

Winged Magic

Barbara Sleigh

Illustrated by John Patience

Share the Love of Reading

Copyright © Barbara Sleigh 1979
Illustrations © Hodder & Stoughton 1979

First published by Hodder & Stoughton
Children's Books 1979
Knight Books edition 1982
This edition produced specially for
School Book Fairs in 1991

British Library C.I.P.

Sleigh, Barbara
  Winged magic
  1. Flight—Legends
  I. Title
  398.2'6   PZ8.1

  ISBN 0 340 26538 8

Printed and bound in Great Britain for Hodder and
Stoughton Paperbacks, a division of Hodder and
Stoughton Ltd., Mill Road, Dunton Green, Sevenoaks,
Kent (Editorial Office: 47 Bedford Square, London, WC1
3DP) by Clays Ltd., St Ives plc.

FOR SIMON

Contents

Five

Once upon a time, an old witch lived in Jamaica. She can't have been a very clever witch, or she would have magicked herself a much better home than the tumbledown hut she lived in. But there it is. Some people are good at one thing and some at another.

Everyone called her just 'Five'. She had been called 'Five' since the oldest grandmother could remember. Nobody knew why. Perhaps because it was safer to hold up five fingers and nod in the direction of her hut, instead of saying her name out loud. You never know with witches.

The old woman hated being called just 'Five'. 'Why can't I have a proper name like everyone else?' she grumbled angrily. 'Five! Why, it doesn't even *mean* a name like Mandy or Poll. I shall make a magic such as no one has ever made before, to stop anyone calling me Five again.'

Now it happened that just then Anansi came along. Anansi was a magic person himself. Sometimes he was a man, and sometimes he was

a spider, but whichever it was, there was always mischief afoot when he was about.

When Anansi came to the witch's hut, he said to himself, 'I wonder what old Five is up to now?' And he peeked through a hole in the wall of the tumbledown house. (Mind you, Anansi was the sort who would *make* a hole in the wall of your house if it suited him.) What should he see but the old witch lighting a fire under her cooking pot and dropping all kinds of horrid things into it. Some were pink and slimy: some had legs, and some were so nasty I don't like to tell you what they were. Well, when she had got the cooking pot full to the brim and bubbling, she screeched out a terrible strong spell, that anyone who said the word 'Five' should drop down dead.

When Anansi heard this, he chuckled to himself. 'This magic is going to be mighty useful for me and my hungry wife and family!' And he tiptoed quietly away.

Next morning he filled a great sack full of yams. (Yams are round and knobbly, like potatoes.) And he heaped them in five piles by the side of the path that everyone used on the way to market. And then he sat down and waited. Presently, along came Mrs Turkey. 'Gibble gubble! Gibble gubble!' Very fat, and high and mighty she was.

'Mrs Turkey, dear Mrs Turkey,' said Anansi. 'Just the very person I hoped I should meet, for I know how clever you are, and how very kind!'

'What can I do to help you, Mr Anansi?' said Mrs Turkey, fluffing out her feathers in a grand way.

'Well,' said Anansi humbly, 'it's like this. I've grown these fine yams, and made them into piles for folks to buy on their way to market, and I'm blessed if I haven't forgotten how to count them!'

'Gibble gubble! Gibble gubble! Nothing could be easier!' said Mrs Turkey, looking down her beak at wicked old Anansi, and she began to count, 'One-gibble, two-gubble, three-gibble, four-gubble . . .' but of course the minute she said 'five', she dropped down dead, and Anansi gobbled her up, every bit, and didn't leave a scrap for his hungry wife and family.

He had only just wiped his mouth and hidden away the feathers, when along came kind Mrs Duck, waddle waddle, 'Quack quack!'

'Oh, Mrs Duck dear,' said Anansi. 'Will you be so good and kind as to count my piles of yams for me? I've quite forgotten how to do it.'

'Quack, quack, of course!' said Mrs Duck. 'Anything to help a friend.' And she began to count, 'One heap, two heaps, three heaps, four heaps . . .' And of course the minute she said 'five' she dropped down dead, and Anansi gobbled her up, every bit. And still he didn't leave a scrap for his hungry wife and family.

He had just wiped his mouth, and hidden all the feathers, feeling rather uncomfortable inside because he had eaten so much, when along came Mrs Dove, pretty, silly Mrs Dove, with her pink feet and snow-white feathers. 'Coo-roo, coo-roo!' said pretty Mrs Dove. 'Of course I'll count your piles of yams for you.' She fluttered up on top of the first heap. 'One!' she cooed: and fluttered up on to the next: 'Two!' she cooed, 'And three – and four . . .' But when she fluttered on to the top of the last heap, she said, 'And the one I am sitting on!'

'That isn't right at all!' said Anansi crossly, for he was feeling very uncomfortable inside because he had eaten so much. 'Count them again!'

So Mrs Dove fluttered back on to the first pile once more. 'One!' she cooed. 'And two! And three! And four! . . . And the one I am sitting on!'

'You silly, stupid Mrs Dove! You don't know how to count at all!' shouted Anansi. And because his too-full inside was hurting so, he quite forgot about the witch's spell, and he bawled out, 'It's one, two, three, four, FIVE!'

And of course, as soon as he said 'five', *he* dropped down dead.

And Mrs Dove flew down from the last pile of yams, and went hopping on to market on her pretty pink feet.

(*From Jamaica*)

The Lyre Bird and the Bubble

Long long ago, even before once upon a time, there were no frogs in Australia. But the streams and the rivers and the waterfalls rolled and splashed and plunged, just as they do today. In them leaped and swirled a host of shining bubbles. And in those bubbles, it was said, lived the Water Spirits, each one in its separate gleaming globe.

Now there was a Lyre Bird who came down to a certain stream to drink. He was given this name because when he spread his tail feathers they looked just like the little harp called a lyre. When he had drunk enough, he would perch on a little hillock near by, spread his tail feathers, lift his beak, and sing. All Lyre Birds are famous for the beauty of their singing, but this Lyre Bird had the most beautiful voice of them all. He sang and sang and sang, so that even the reeds stopped their rustling to listen; and the bubbles, each with its Water Spirit inside, would swirl and dance and sparkle in the sunshine to his singing, until it was time for them to sail on down the stream.

14

Now there was one bubble which turned and twirled and danced with the others, but it did not sail away with them. It was always there when the Lyre Bird came down to drink, bobbing gently up and down in the same place, between a reed and a pebble. But no sooner did the Lyre Bird begin to sing his song than it leaped in the air, as if in greeting, before twirling and twizzling in the water with the other bubbles.

Unknown to the Lyre Bird, this bubble was the home of a Water Spirit on whom his singing had worked a magic. So enchanted was it by the Lyre Bird's song that it began to wish to burst from its bubble into the open air and the sunshine, and become, not a Spirit, but a solid, living creature, so that it could learn to sing as beautifully as the Lyre Bird.

The Spirit went on wishing and wishing inside its bubble, until one day a tiny green speck appeared at its heart. The speck grew larger and larger, turning faster and faster to the singing of the Lyre Bird, until it completely filled the shell of its shining bubble. When there was no more room for it to grow, one morning, as the Lyre Bird sang its longest, highest note, the bubble popped – and out hopped a small green *frog*. The first frog in the world.

It sat on a stone with its green toes turned in, and its golden goggle eyes gazing up at the Lyre Bird.

'Go on! Go on making that beautiful sound!' begged the Frog, for the Lyre Bird had stopped singing in surprise. So the Lyre Bird sang on. But when he came to the end of his song, the Frog said, 'What *is* that wonderful noise you make with your beak?'

'It is called "singing",' said the Lyre Bird.

'What would I not give to be able to make this "singing"!' said the Frog.

'Then I will teach you,' said the Lyre Bird. 'You must begin by opening your mouth as wide as it will go. Then, you take a deep breath, and let it out again, all the time *thinking* the note you want to sing.'

The Frog opened his mouth and breathed out, and thought and thought and thought. But, try as he would, no sound came.

'Again! Again!' cried the Lyre Bird. And at last, from his yellow throat came one tiny musical note, and he was so pleased with himself that he jumped up and down on his stone singing the same sound over and over again. Each time it was a little louder.

Every day the Lyre Bird taught him another note, then another and another, until the Frog could sing high and low, loud and soft, with trills and flourishes.

'How beautifully I sing!' he chanted. 'I should like all the world to hear me!'

16

So the Lyre Bird, who was proud of his pupil, sent for all the animals in Australia: the kangaroo, the koala and the cassowary, the wombat and the wallaby, every creature that runs and jumps and hops and crawls.

As it was the first Frog in the world, they had never seen anything like it before. When they saw this strange little creature, with its goggle eyes, and legs cramped crooked by the lack of space in the bubble, they began to laugh; and the poor Frog sat on his stone with hanging head.

'Peace! Peace!' called the Lyre Bird above the noise of their merriment, 'I called you here to listen, not to laugh. Sing to them, Frogling. Sing!'

So the Frog lifted up his head, and opened his wide mouth, and the song he sang was so beautiful that one by one the animals stopped laughing, until the whole company was still.

'We have heard of *birds* that sing,' they said. 'But never a creature that goes on four feet. Why, he sings as beautifully as the Lyre Bird himself!' And at this the Frog's proud smile grew very wide indeed.

But when evening came, and the animals slipped away, and the Lyre Bird had gone about his business, he sat all alone on his stone, and two tears trickled from his golden eyes.

'What does it matter whether I sing well or ill, if there is no one to hear me?' he sighed.

Now, the Great Spirit heard his sad moaning, and said, 'You shall not be alone. Every creature has a mate, and you shall have one too.'

And so he gave the Frog a little green frog wife, and he sang to her, morning, noon and night.

He was too proud to listen to the Lyre Bird any longer.

'How lucky you are to be my wife!' he said one evening as the moon was rising. 'Did not all the animals in Australia come to hear my singing? Who cares for the song of the Lyre Bird when *I* can sing to them? Why, if I wish, I could sing the moon out of the sky!'

'Could you really?' said his wife. 'I should dearly like the moon to play with!' And she gazed up at him hopefully. (To tell the truth, she was getting rather tired of all this singing.)

By now the Frog had grown so conceited that he really believed what he was saying. 'The moon to play with?' he cried. 'Then you shall have it, my dear.' And he lifted his head in the white moonshine, and opened his wide mouth as wide as it would go.

Now the Great Spirit had heard his boasting, and his ingratitude to the Lyre Bird. 'It is time that this small animal was taught a lesson,' he said to himself, and although the Frog opened his mouth so wide, and took such a deep breath, the moon took not a bit of notice, but went on sailing across the sky. For, instead of a song, all that came out of the Frog's wide throat was a dismal – 'Croak!'

And from that day to this, a croak is the only sound that all the frogs in the world can make.

(*From Australia*)

Prince Shaggy-Legs

Very many years ago, there was a King of Sweden who had a little daughter called Thora. He loved her dearly. Nothing, he thought, was too good for Princess Thora. Her skipping-rope was made of crimson silk, with silver handles, and her whipping-top of ivory.

One day, when the King was coming home from hunting, he saw two small lizard-like creatures, curled up asleep on a sun-baked rock. He stopped, and looked at them with surprise. Their scales gleamed green in the evening sun; down the back of each one, from head to pointed tail, ran a row of tiny spikes, between a pair of wings no bigger than a robin's. The King smiled at the little creatures. 'Never before have I seen a pair of lizards with wings. I will take them home for Princess Thora to play with,' he said, and he ordered one of the huntsmen to pick them up and carry them back to the castle.

The huntsman noticed a wisp of smoke curling from the lizards' small nostrils, and though the tiny paws bunched under each chin as they slept were no bigger than those of a dormouse, the claws which grew from them looked as sharp as needles.

'Come, come! What are you waiting for?' asked his master. And, as kings must be obeyed, the huntsman picked up one of the lizards and dropped it into his leather hunting-cap. The smoke from its nostrils made him sneeze. When he picked up the second lizard it writhed and wriggled, and hissing angrily, gave his thumb a sharp nip, which drew blood even through his leather glove.

The King looked down at the lizards with smiling eyes, but the lizards looked up at the King from the bottom of the huntsman's cap

with eyes that glowed like live coals. There was a slight smell of singeing leather. 'We shall see if the Princess will tame them,' said the King.

But Princess Thora did not tame them. She said, 'Thank you', politely to her father, when he tipped the little creatures on to the floor beside her. But when they skittered round her feet, growling and nuzzling at her toes, she jumped up on a stool. And when they rose in the air on their tiny leathery wings, swooping and swirling round her ears, she picked up the hem of her wide skirt and pulled it over her head, in case they should get entangled in her golden hair. And her ladies ran shrieking from the room.

Then the King stopped laughing. 'Ho there, men-at-arms!' he called. 'Catch me those lizard creatures! But do them no harm.'

The men-at-arms tried in vain to round them up, for the breath from the lizards' nostrils set them coughing and sneezing till the tears ran down their cheeks.

After a long chase, the two little creatures took refuge at the back of the fire burning on the great hearth, without any care for the heat, which drove back the men-at-arms.

'These are very strange lizards!' said the King.

'Perhaps they are cross because they are hungry,' said Princess Thora. 'If we feed them it may be we shall tame them.'

So she jumped down from the stool, and ran and fetched a dish of bread-and-milk, which she set down beside the hearth. 'When we have all gone away for the night perhaps they will come out and eat.'

The next morning, the bread-and-milk was still there – but Princess Thora's pet mouse was not. Something that looked very like a mouse's tail lay by the dish, and the lizards looked a little fatter.

The morning after that, all that could be found of Princess Thora's white kitten was a handful of draggled fur on the hearth. The lizards looked fatter still, and their eyes smouldered, red with malice. But Thora's eyes were red with weeping for her pets. Then, and only then, did the King realise that what he had thought were lizards were baby dragons.

But little dragons grow into big dragons, so what was he to do with them?

'I dare not turn them out of doors,' he said. 'They have already eaten a mouse and a cat. As they grow bigger, perhaps next it will be a dog, then a goat, or a sheep, then a horse or a cow –'

'Or even people!' said Princess Thora anxiously.

And so the King ordered a great iron cage to be built in the castle courtyard. When it was finished, and it took some days, six men-at-arms prodded the dragons out from the back of the hearth with their sharp spears. And when the creatures rose in the air and circled the room with flapping wings, six more men-at-arms threw a great net over them, though nearly fainting with the dragons' poisonous breath. In this way they were caught and locked in the iron cage.

And that, you might think, was that. But not a bit of it.

The dragons were a good deal bigger now, and the next morning the bars of the cage had become so twisted by the heat of their breath, that they had been able to escape. They had flown to the mountains outside the city. There they found a cave, in which they made their home.

Time went by, until both dragons and Princess became fully grown. But whereas Princess Thora was now as brave and beautiful as you would expect a princess to be, the dragons were huge and horrible. They had become the terror of the countryside. Their poisonous breath shrivelled and withered every green thing within range. It even paralysed the brave men who went out to fight them. Everyone touched by the horrible blast fell fainting to the ground, unable to defend himself against the monsters' huge teeth and claws. Nothing would satisfy their hunger but an ox or a cow apiece, a couple of human beings, or half a dozen small children.

The King was in despair. He promised the hand of Princess Thora in marriage to any man who would rid the country of the terrible creatures. Many came forward, for the fame of the beauty of Princess Thora had spread far and wide. But either they turned and ran at the first sight of the two monsters, or else the dragons made short work of them while they lay stupefied by the venom of their breath, for which there seemed no defence, for its vapours seeped through every chink of their chain-mail.

Now, there was a brave prince of neighbouring Denmark called Ragnar, who fell in love with the beautiful Princess Thora, and she with him. Prince Ragnar was determined to kill the two dragons and win the Princess. 'Strength and courage are not enough,' he said to himself. 'Somehow the creatures must be outwitted.'

After some thought, he had a suit of clothes made with a lining which was stuffed with wool. Over this he wore trousers of goat-skin, with the fur on the outside. He reached Sweden just before nightfall, and straightway plunged into a lake. When his strange garments were thoroughly soaked with water, he climbed from the lake and stood in the freezing cold, so that by morning they were frozen to solid ice thicker than any armour. The fur of his goatskin trousers stood out in points, as sharp as daggers. Armed only with spear and shield he went off to meet the dragons as soon as the sun rose. The King and his courtiers and Princess Thora and all the townspeople who were left, stood on a hill at a safe distance to watch what would happen.

'Ho there, dragons!' shouted Prince Ragnar. 'Come out and fight!'

Out of their cave the two huge creatures came, their great wings spread wide, roaring and hissing as they raced towards him, their scales flashing blue and gold through the mist of foul breath that swirled towards Prince Ragnar. So frightened were the King and the townspeople at the sight that they turned and fled. Only Princess Thora stood, and watched, and waited.

But Ragnar was ready for the dragons. He stood his ground, with his shield before his face, knowing that no breath, however loathsome, could penetrate his icy armour. The two dragons reared up in surprise that he did not fall grovelling on the ground, and during the brief moment when they breathed in, before breathing out yet again a blast of poisonous vapour, Prince Ragnar took aim and hurled his spear with such skill that it pierced the hearts of both dragons at one blow. Even threshing on the ground in their death agony, they could not penetrate his icy armour with their fearful claws. Soon, they lay lifeless at

his feet, and the last trace of their horrible breath drifted away in the morning air.

The King and his courtiers and all the towns-people ran out to greet the Prince, and you may be sure that Princess Thora ran faster than any of them.

Now, by this time, the warmth of the sun had

melted the ice that had been Prince Ragnar's protection. In his sodden clothes and dripping goat-skin he looked a very strange sight. The King laughed, and cried as he ran to greet him. 'Praise and welcome to the conqueror, Prince Ragnar *Shaggy-Legs*!'

And all the people took up the cry: 'Welcome, Prince Ragnar Shaggy-Legs!'

So Princess Thora married Ragnar Shaggy-Legs (for so he was always known, with great affection), and when her father died he became King of Sweden in his place.

(From Sweden)

A Wreath of Wild Roses

Once upon a time, there was a woodcutter, who had two daughters. Both had blue eyes, and rosy cheeks, and golden hair when they were little girls, but as they grew up, Maria became bad-tempered and sour as a green apple, so that her face was covered with cross-patch wrinkles; and because she was too lazy to brush it, her hair looked grey and dusty and hung down like a wet mop. If everyone called her ugly, it was entirely her own fault. But her sister, Mariette, was as pretty as a clean cheerful willing face could make her.

One day, when the woodcutter came home from work, he said, 'Bless my buttons if I haven't left my axe behind in the forest. Now I shall have to go all the way back to fetch it, and me with a great blister on my heel!'

'Don't worry, father,' said Mariette, 'I'll go and fetch it for you.' And she gave him a kiss and set out, while Maria just scowled, and hid herself so that no one should ask her to go too.

29

Mariette had barely started on her walk when the rain came down like silver needles; so she put her old shawl over her head, and jumped over the puddles as well as she could. By the time she reached the clearing where she knew her father had been working, the rain had stopped and the sun came out. There she saw the axe, fixed in the stump of a tree. On the handle perched two snow-white doves, who were wet and shivering with cold. 'Coo-coo-roo!' cooed the doves unhappily. 'Coo-coo-roo!'

'You poor little birds!' said Mariette, and she dried their feathers with her shawl, and warmed them between her hands. Then she fed them with the crust she had kept to cheer herself on her long walk home. When they had pecked up every crumb, a little dwarf, dressed all in yellow, stepped from behind a bush, and with a whirr of white wings the doves flew on to his shoulders, cooing excitedly in his pointed ears. 'Coo-coo-roo!' they cried. 'Coo-coo-roo!'

The little man listened, nodding from time to time, and when they had finished he said to Mariette: 'What can I give you as a reward for your kindness to my doves?'

'But I want no reward,' she replied.

'May be,' said the Yellow Dwarf. 'But my doves and I would like to give you something. What shall it be, my dear?'

Mariette thought the little man looked as poor as she was herself, and could ill afford to give her anything. But as she did not want to hurt his feelings, she looked hurriedly round and said, after a pause, 'I should like – a wreath of wild roses!'

With surprising speed, the Yellow Dwarf picked some strands of the wild roses which hung from the branches of a bush, and with strange flickering movements of his hands wove them into a wreath, and held it out to her.

'How beautiful!' said Mariette, holding it up.

'It is no ordinary wreath,' said the Dwarf. 'Look closely, my dear.'

Then Mariette saw that, perched among the flowers, were dozens of tiny blue birds, no bigger than her thimble.

'Sing, little blue birds! Sing!' cried the Dwarf, and the tiny creatures lifted up their golden bills and sang as sweetly as the nightingale when the moon is full.

Mariette laughed with pleasure, and put the wreath on her head. Then she thanked the Yellow Dwarf, put the axe over her shoulder, and went skipping home. And the wreath sang to her all the way, so that it seemed no distance at all.

When at last she reached the woodcutter's hut, and Maria saw the rosy wreath, and heard the sweet singing of the tiny birds, she said, 'I want a wreath that sings!' And she grabbed the wreath and put it on. But no sooner had she settled it on her tousled hair, than the wild roses began to fade and drop their pink petals, while the little birds turned to buzzing bluebottles.

'It's a *horrid* wreath!' grumbled Maria, pulling it off her head and flinging it on the floor. 'I shall go to the forest myself, and I expect the Yellow Dwarf will give me something much more grand.' And, after kicking the faded wreath into a corner, off she went. But when Mariette picked up the wreath and put it on again, at once the

32

drooping roses lifted their heads and bloomed, and the bluebottles ceased their buzzing and became little singing blue birds again.

When Maria reached the clearing in the forest, she was even more bad-tempered than usual, for she had borrowed Mariette's Sunday shoes, and they were much too tight. When she saw the white doves perched upon the tree-stump, she cried, 'Get away, you stupid creatures! *I* want to sit there!' And she flapped them away and sat down. Then she kicked off her tight shoes, and waggled her ugly great toes, and began to eat a slab of plum-cake she had brought with her.

The doves looked on with their bright eyes, and hopped round expectantly, but instead of crumbs, Maria threw first one shoe and then the other at the poor birds, crying as she did so, 'Do you think I have carried a great heavy piece of cake all this way, just to feed a lot of silly birds? Get away, you greedy guzzlers!' And the doves flew sadly away.

'I wish that dwarf would hurry up,' went on Maria. 'I want my reward.'

'And you shall have your reward!' said the Yellow Dwarf, stepping suddenly from behind a tree. 'I saw it all. "Greedy guzzlers" you called my doves, so from now on those shall be the only words you can say!'

Maria thought of all kinds of rude things to say

to him in reply, but it was no use. The only words that came from her lips were – 'Greedy guzzlers!'

When she reached home, she gargled and rubbed her throat till it was sore both inside and out, but it made no difference: she could still only say, 'Greedy guzzlers!'

Now the fame of the wreath that sang, and the beauty of the girl who wore it, soon spread abroad, and who should come to see for himself, one day, but the King's son. As soon as he saw Mariette's lovely face, he fell in love with her and asked her to be his wife. They were married in the great cathedral, and all the choir fell silent at the singing of the little blue birds, and the carved saints turned their stone heads to listen.

You would expect me to say that they both lived happily ever after. And so they would have done if it had not been for Maria, who was eaten up with jealousy. Although all she could still *say* was, 'Greedy guzzlers!' she *thought* to herself, 'Why should Mariette live in a King's palace, and wear a golden gown, while I live in a poor hut, in nothing but rags?' And she went on thinking this until a wicked plan came into her head. She had often been told by her father how she and Mariette had once been so alike. Supposing she brushed her hair and tried really hard to look pleasant, could she make herself look as pretty as Mariette? She fetched her sister's hairbrush, and, standing in front of the little cracked mirror, which was all she had, she brushed and brushed until, gradually, the dust of weeks came away, and her hair began to shine almost as brightly as Mariette's had done. Next, she tried looking pleasant. This was a great deal harder. But she smirked and ogled at herself in the mirror until her mouth began to turn up at the corners, and only if you looked closely could you see the crosspatch wrinkles. And at last she really did begin to look like Mariette.

Then she ran as fast as she could to the palace. When she saw Mariette feeding the peacocks on the terrace, the sight of the splendour in which her sister now lived caused Maria to look for a moment as cross as she had ever done, so that Mariette had no difficulty in recognising her. She was delighted to see her again, and loaded her with presents.

Then she asked her what she would like most to do. Just remembering in time not to speak, Maria made signs that there was nothing she would like better on such a hot day than to bathe. Mariette agreed. And so they made their way to the palace lake, which lay in the middle of a ring of trees. But no sooner had Mariette slipped off her golden gown, than Maria took her by the shoulders and pushed her into the water. Then she picked up the singing wreath, and threw it after her. And both Mariette and the wreath sank beneath the still waters of the lake. Twittering sadly, the blue birds flew away.

Then Maria crowed with glee, and after changing her ragged skirt for Mariette's golden gown, she smoothed her hair and, smirking cheerfully, made her way to the palace, pushing rudely past the servants and sometimes, forgetting that she must hold her tongue, calling the courtiers, 'Greedy guzzlers', to their great surprise.

When the Prince found that though his Princess looked much the same as usual her manners had become rude and rough, he was sadly troubled. 'What is the matter, my dear?' he asked. 'And why will you not speak to me? Are you ill?'

But Maria knew better than to try to answer. So the Prince sent for the wisest doctors in the land. But they could find no cure for her silence or her rude, rough behaviour. All she would do was to eat, and throw things at the servants.

Weeks went by, and the Prince grew pale and thin, for he had loved his gentle wife. One day, as he sat silent in his garden, he thought he saw a cloud of tiny blue butterflies, which hovered over the rosebush beneath which he was sitting. Suddenly they began to sing – as sweetly as the nightingale when the moon is full. Now butterflies do not sing, so the Prince started up, and recognised at once the little blue birds. 'Tell me,' he said, 'what has happened to the singing wreath? And what can I do to change my Princess back to the gentle wife I loved so well?'

All at once, the blue birds darted off like dragonflies, and the Prince followed. They led him to the lake, where they hovered over the water as though they were waiting for something. As he watched, he saw the water stir and dimple, and, through a ring of shining ripples, rose the real Princess, with the wreath upon her head.

'Dear husband!' cried Mariette. 'My jealous sister pushed me into the lake and threw the wreath after me. She did not know that as long as I wear it I can live an enchanted life beneath the water.'

'She looks like you, and wears your clothes, but there the likeness ends,' said the Prince. 'Dear wife, what can I do to break this watery spell and bring you back again?'

'Listen well, my dear,' replied Mariette. 'For I must return to the mud and ooze at the bottom of the lake. When I sink once more beneath the water, you will find the singing wreath floating on the surface. Take it quickly to the palace, and put it on the head of my cruel sister, and you will see her as she really is.'

'What then?' asked the Prince.

'If you wish to save me,' said Mariette, 'before

the sun sets, you must dive to the bottom of the lake. There, in the mud, you will see a hideous great slug. Take it in your arms and carry it to the shore. Remember, whatever it may turn into, hold it fast, or you will never see me again. Above all, make haste. Once the sun has set I can live no longer under the water without the singing wreath.'

As she spoke, Mariette sank once more into the lake. Only the ripples showed where she had been. And there, on the surface, floated the singing wreath. It drifted to the bank where the Prince stood. He took it up, and the tiny blue birds settled among the roses, singing joyfully. Then he hurried to the palace, and who should come to meet him but Maria, elbowing her way through the courtiers. Before she could prevent him, he put the wreath on her head. At once, the roses began to droop, and when Maria saw their fading petals falling to the ground, and heard the singing of the blue birds turn to the buzzing of angry bluebottles, she was so furious that her mouth turned down at the corners, and all the crosspatch wrinkles creased her face again so that she looked as ugly as she had ever done. By the Prince's horrified face she realised she had been discovered, and, flinging the wreath on the floor, she turned and fled for her life, and was never seen again.

Then the Prince saw that the rim of the sun was just beginning to sink behind a bank of purple cloud, and he ran to the lake as fast as he could go. By the time he came to the wood, a quarter of the sun had sunk behind the cloud. When he reached the lake and dived into the water, only half the crimson circle could be seen.

Down, down he went, to the bottom of the lake, and there, as Mariette had said, he found a hideous great slug. Steeling himself to touch the horrible slimy thing, he shut his eyes and, clasping it in his arms, fought his way up again. Suddenly, he found he was holding not a slug, but a serpent, whose coils twisted themselves round him in such a grip that he could scarcely move.

But he held it fast. Just as he reached the surface the serpent changed into a great bird, whose wings were made of iron and whose beak was of steel, with which it attacked the Prince. But still he held fast, and as he stumbled ashore, the spell was broken, the bird was gone, and in its place was his own dear wife, Mariette. And at that very minute the last of the sun disappeared behind the purple cloud.

Then Mariette and the Prince walked back to the palace hand in hand, in great joy and contentment.

And, this time, they really *did* live happily ever after.

(*From France*)

Small is often Clever

Once upon a time there was a wasp, who lived with her friend Crab, not on the seashore, as you might expect, but in a hole, at the foot of a cherry tree at the bottom of a mountain. They kept their hole as neat and tidy as any hole in all Japan, for that is where they lived.

One day, when the cherry tree was hung with pink blossom, Crab, who was sweeping the dust from the door, called out, 'Wasp! Wasp! Come quickly! Just look what I have found lying on the grass outside: a pile of rice, all ready cooked! How can it have got there?'

'Rice?' said Wasp. 'Dropped, no doubt, by the traveller who stopped to rest in the shade of the cherry tree this morning. It will make a very tasty supper for us both. I will fetch a bowl to put it in.'

While Crab was waiting for Wasp to come back with the bowl, a monkey, who lived in a near-by tree, came to see why she was waving her claws about in such an excited way.

'Rice?' he said. '*Cooked* rice? Why, that is my favourite supper! I tell you what, friend Crab: in exchange for the rice, I will give you the stone of the peach I have just eaten. I never tasted such a juicy peach in my life!'

Now Crab was a simple soul. She looked at the stone, which seemed very dry, however juicy the peach may have been. She waved her claws in an undecided way, but by the time she had made up her mind that it would be a poor exchange for the rice, Monkey had crammed every grain in his mouth, without a word of thanks.

Wasp came rolling the bowl along, just in time to see him swinging himself away from branch to branch, and laughing his head off. 'I'll give him peach stone!' she buzzed angrily, when Crab explained what had happened. 'Just you wait, you wicked monkey!' she zizzed. 'Just because you are big and we are small, you may think you can do what you like with us. But one day we shall get the better of you!'

Early next morning, Monkey went to visit an aunt who lived on the other side of the mountain, so Wasp and Crab did not see him again until the blossom had faded from the tree and it was hung instead with glowing red cherries, like a hundred crab-sized lanterns.

Very polite Monkey was this time, when he found Crab sunning herself outside her own

41

front door. 'Good day to you, Madam Crab!' he said. 'I trust you are well? And all at home? I suppose you couldn't spare a few cherries for a poor starving animal?'

Crab put her head on one side, and looked at Monkey with surprise.

'You seem very plump, for a starving monkey,' she said. 'But there, things are not always what they seem. If you are hungry, you are welcome to some of our cherries. But I beg you, do not think me rude if I don't offer to pick them for you. For though I am thought to have an excellent figure – for a crab, that is – it is not the best shape for climbing trees.'

'Think nothing of it, dear madam,' said the monkey, waving his paws airily. 'Would you allow me to climb the tree myself? Then I could pick the cherries and throw them down to you. Just one or two, perhaps, I could keep for myself?' And without waiting for Crab to agree, he scampered up the tree, and began picking the ripest cherries as fast as he could, and cramming them in to his wide mouth.

Now Crab was not so simple that she had not felt a little uneasy at his suggestion, and she was just going in search of her friend to ask her advice when Wasp flew down from the tall grass on which she had been sitting, with an angry zizz. 'I heard it all, my poor silly Crab,' she said. 'That

Monkey is a rogue and a cheat! But leave it all to me: we shall be even with him yet. For the moment, we will just watch.'

What they saw made Wasp zizz even more angrily. For when Monkey had crammed as much fruit in his mouth as it would hold, he spat out the stones, which rattled down on poor Crab so that her shell ached and her claws tingled and she groaned aloud. Then, he crammed all the rest of the ripe fruit in his pockets. At last, he called out, 'And now you shall have your share, Mrs Crab!' And as he spoke, he shook down the few cherries that were left, all of which were green, and sour, and hard as the cherry stones themselves.

Wasp watched all this with wings quivering with rage. 'Now, leave everything to me!' she whispered to the unhappy Crab.

Aloud, she went on sweetly, 'Sir Monkey, never did I see a tree climbed with such speed, and so gracefully! I have often heard how clever you and your brothers are at turning head over heels among the branches. I suppose that, after eating so many cherries, you would not be able to show us how you do it?'

'Nothing could be easier, dear Madam Wasp!' said Monkey, with a grin, for there was nothing he liked better than showing off. So, taking hold of a branch of the cherry tree, he swung himself round and round. Over and over he went, but every time he flew over the branch, the cherries fell in a shower out of his pockets on the grass beneath. And as fast as they fell, Crab picked them up and piled them by the hole that was their front door.

Presently, when Monkey had swung himself quite giddy, he jumped down from the tree, laughing at his own cleverness.

But when he saw the pile of ripe cherries, with Wasp sitting on top, zizzing angrily, with quivering wings, and Crab standing in front snapping her claws, he stopped laughing. And when he felt in his pockets and found them quite empty, except for one squashed cherry, he bristled with rage.

'Tricked!' he shouted. 'And by two such feeble creatures as a crab and a wasp! I shall make you pay for this!' And he made a dive at the pile of cherries, hoping to steal some of them back even now. But Wasp flew round and round him so fast that he could not see her, but only hear her zizz, now here, now there. Flap his paws how he would, he could not manage to swat her. What with this, and Crab snapping her claws so valiantly, he felt he had better go, and quickly.

'*So* kind of you to pick our cherries for us!' cried Wasp with a grin, as he turned and ran. Away went Monkey to the other side of the

mountain, to see what his aunt had cooked for supper – vowing vengeance in his heart, for no one likes to be laughed at by a wasp.

When he had gone, Wasp put Crab to bed, for her poor shell was sore from the hail of cherry stones, and zizzed her to sleep with a lullaby. It was no use asking her what they should do next, so Wasp left her sleeping. She said to herself, 'We must be ready to defend ourselves against this wicked Monkey, for surely he will come back again.' Presently she thought of a plan.

First thing next morning, she lit the fire.

Then she put an egg in a corner of the hearth.

Next, she balanced a hammer on top of the door, which she left half-open.

Last of all, she put a basin of water in a corner.

And Crab? She was still in bed, resting her poor shell. But she pulled the blankets up in a heap so that only her eyes showed over the top. Then they both waited.

Presently, who should come knocking on the door but Monkey. 'Dear Madam Crab?' he called. 'Sweet Mistress Wasp? Are you at home?'

There was no answer, so he poked his head round the door.

'Is there anyone about?' he cried. And as there was still no answer, he tiptoed inside and looked round him. 'I wonder where they have hidden those delicious ripe cherries? The very thought of them makes my mouth water!'

But all there was to be seen was:

An egg on the hearth.

A basin of water in a corner.

A pile of old blankets on a bed.

(He did not notice the hammer on top of the door.)

'An egg!' said Monkey, licking his chops. 'Next to cooked rice and ripe cherries, there is nothing I like so much! But first I think I will put it on the fire to cook.'

Very carefully, he picked up the egg and placed it on the glowing embers. But, as soon as the shell grew hot, it burst into a thousand pieces, which flew in his face.

'My poor scratched face!' he moaned. 'Perhaps if I bathe it in that basin of water it will not hurt so much.' But when he bent over the basin, Wasp flew out and stung him, now here, now there, so that he begged for mercy. 'Help! Help! I must get away from here!' he cried.

But as he dashed through the door, the hammer fell on top of him, so that he ran off groaning. And his head was still humming, like a whole nest full of wasps, when he reached his aunt who lived on the other side of the mountain.

That was the last that Wasp and Crab ever saw of Monkey.

They both lived happily ever after in the hole, at the foot of the cherry tree, in Japan.

(From Japan)

The Tower of Brass

Once upon a time there was a Rajah who was the richest prince in all India. His palace was paved with gold, and his chariots were so studded with jewels that his enemies were dazzled by them when he went to war.

Now, this Rajah was so used to having his own way, that if anyone dared to question his commands he would fly into a rage, and inflict the most terrible punishments on the unhappy offender. Only one man dared to shake his head when he was commanded to carry out some wrong or foolish command, and that was his Chief Minister. But the time came when even he fell into disgrace.

'Why do you hinder and thwart me at every turn?' thundered the Rajah.

'Indeed, my lord,' said the Chief Minister, humbly, 'I only try to hinder you from actions on which the gods will frown, or that would be whispered and laughed over in the bazaar.'

'*What*!' roared the Rajah. 'Do you dare suggest

that *anyone* would dare to laugh at *me*? For that insult you shall be punished. Guards! Seize this traitor, lock him in the Brass Tower, and bring me the key!' And turning to the unhappy man, he went on, 'What have you to say to that?'

'Only that for all his riches a man may be poor if there is nó one near him he can trust,' answered the Minister.

'Do you suggest that I am *poor*?' shouted the Rajah. 'For that final impudence you shall not only be imprisoned in the Brass Tower, but you shall be given neither food nor water. Take him away!'

The Brass Tower stood outside the city, on a hill, with not a single tree to give it shelter. When the mid-day sun poured down, its walls grew so hot that, to be a prisoner there, meant certain death. From a distance it seemed to quiver in the heat, so that it had the reputation of being enchanted. Few people would go near it, and so it was thought there was no need to set a guard at its single gate.

Now the Chief Minister had a wife called Dorani, who loved him as dearly as he loved her. When her husband failed to come home, she became alarmed, and sent a servant to find out what had happened to him. When at last the servant returned, she saw by his troubled face that something evil had happened.

'Tell me quickly what you have discovered,' she said. 'However hard it may be to hear.'

'I went to the Palace,' said the servant, 'but nobody there would speak to me. They turned their eyes away as if they were afraid. So then I went to the bazaar, where the gossip is, and there it was being whispered that my Lord has been imprisoned in the Brass Tower, without food or water.'

'May the gods have mercy on him!' prayed Dorani. But she did not just sit at home, wringing her hands. Pulling her veil over her face, she slipped out of the courtyard, and ran and ran until, all breathless and footsore, she came to the foot of the Brass Tower, just as the sun was setting. Through a narrow window at the top of the tower she could see her husband breathing in the cool air for the sun made his brass-walled prison unbearable.

'My Lord! It is I! Dorani, your wife! What can I do to help you in your distress?'

'There is indeed something you can do, light of my eyes,' he replied. 'Tomorrow morning, bring me sixty yards of the finest silk, sixty yards of strong cotton, sixty yards of twine, and sixty yards of rope. Bring me also a beetle.'

'A *beetle*?' cried Dorani in astonishment.

'Do not stay to question why,' said her husband, 'but see that the beetle is *strong*, and *hungry*.'

'But how can I bring sixty yards of silk, sixty yards of cotton, sixty yards of twine, and sixty yards of rope, without arousing suspicion?' said Dorani.

'Wind each one in turn around your waist,' he replied, 'and arrange your sari over them. That way, no one will notice anything unusual. One more request: besides these things, bring me a single drop of honey.'

'But a single drop of honey will be of no use to your hunger!' said Dorani in dismay.

'Do as I ask without questioning,' said her husband. 'Do not fail me, for I cannot live another day in the Brass Tower. Make haste, I beg you!'

'I will not fail you,' said Dorani. 'I shall run so fast that my feet will not bend a single blade of grass.'

And so she hurried away. Next morning she had no difficulty in finding sixty yards of silk, sixty yards of cotton, sixty yards of twine, and sixty yards of rope. The drop of honey she put ready in a tiny ivory box. But not until the sun was hot on the ground did the insects seem to stir. There seemed to be beetles of every size and colour, red, blue and yellow: which should she choose? Some of them looked strong, and some of them looked so frail that it was a wonder their legs could carry them. How could she discover which of them were hungry?

At last, seeing how greedily each went from flower to flower, Dorani said to herself, 'If I catch a beetle now, and keep him close, so that he cannot feed, surely by midday he will be a very hungry beetle indeed!'

As she said this to herself, a stout-looking beetle circled round her, on shining green wings, and landed on the very flower she was twisting in her anxious fingers. Quickly she clapped her other hand over both flower and beetle. The little creature buzzed angrily, but Dorani said softly, 'Forgive me, my friend! But when my master is rescued you shall be well rewarded, and I promise you shall go free.'

Whether the beetle understood or not, he stopped his angry buzzing, tucked all his feet beneath him and lay still in the palm of her hand.

Then Dorani wound round her waist the sixty yards of silk, the sixty yards of cotton, the sixty yards of twine, and the sixty yards of rope, and arranged her sari over them. Next she tucked the little box of ivory with the honey inside, into the folds at her waist, and carrying the green beetle between her two cupped hands she hurried to the Brass Tower. Far above her she could see her husband gazing anxiously from the window at the top of the Tower.

'My lord!' she cried. 'I have brought everything you asked for, the silk, the cotton, the twine, the rope, the beetle and the honey: but how can I give them to you?'

'Do as I tell you,' he called down. 'First unwind the silk, the cotton, the twine and the rope.'

So twirling like a top Dorani unwound them from her waist, so that they lay in a neat coil at her feet.

'Now tie one end of the rope to one end of the twine; then tie the other end of the twine to one end of the cotton and the other end of the cotton to one end of the silk.'

'But what shall I do with the other end of the silk?' asked Dorani.

'Tie it securely to the beetle. Having done that, put the drop of honey on the end of the beetle's nose – only on the end of his nose – and if you value my life put the creature very carefully on the wall of the tower facing upwards, so that smelling the honey always in front, it will climb and climb to the top of the Tower, bringing the end of the silk with him.'

Then Dorani laughed aloud at the cleverness of her husband. When she had done exactly as she was bidden she watched the beetle half scramble, half fly up the wall of the tower in his anxiety to get at the honey he could smell in front of him. Up and up it went until she could no longer see

53

the little green speck. Only the unwinding of the coil of silk at her feet showed that it was still on its upward journey. When the knot of silk and cotton began to follow in its turn, at twice the speed, she knew that the beetle had reached the top of the tower, and that her husband himself was hauling it up, and that it would be followed by the twine, until the end of the precious rope was in his hands with which he could make his escape.

At last, with the end of the rope tied to the grille of the window, he let himself down, hand under hand, until at last he reached the ground and the loving arms of Dorani his wife.

'And the little beetle?' she asked, when he had embraced her.

'In the folds of my sash,' said her husband. 'When we are safely at home he shall have as much honey as he can eat.'

So hand in hand they returned, and Dorani hid her husband, so that not even the servants knew their master had returned.

Now as so often happened, the Rajah soon began to repent of his anger. More and more he missed his Chief Minister, and longed for his honest advice. At last he said, 'I cannot bring him back to life, but I can at least bury his bones with honour.'

So he gave the key of the Brass Tower to his

servants, and ordered them to bring his corpse back to the palace.

Imagine his surprise when he heard that the prisoner had escaped!

When the Chief Minister heard of his master's change of heart – for such news travels fast – he came to the Rajah, who hailed him with joy. When he heard how the escape had been made, he laughed heartily. Then he said, 'My friend, your story proves only too well the great truth of the words for which you were so sorely punished. The worth of someone who can be trusted is beyond the price of riches, whether it be found in a Chief Minister, a wife, or – even a little green beetle!'

(*From India*)

The Tale of Little Half-Chick

Once upon a time there was a little Spanish hen who boasted that her feathers were the blackest in the hen-yard; that her comb was the most charming pink; and her legs the most beautiful yellow.

'And when I hatch my five brown eggs, they will be the finest chickens that the farm-yard has ever seen,' she clucked.

The other hens did not care for this sort of talk at all, but when the first chicken was hatched they had to admit it was a fine little bird, and so was the second, and the third. By the time the fourth appeared, the little black hen was so conceited that she could hardly bring herself to lower her beak to peck her morning corn. When the fifth little chicken stepped from its broken shell, she did not bother to look down, until one of the other hens began to cluck with laughter, and another, and another, until the whole farm-yard was clacking and crowing with merriment, and the farmer's wife ran out to see if a fox had got into the yard. When she saw the fifth chick, she too began to laugh.

'Come and see!' she called to her husband. 'Our little black hen has hatched a half-chicken! It is just as though he has been split in two and the other half has got lost! For he has only one leg, one wing, one eye, and half a beak! But he looks a cheeky little fellow, for all that.'

Then, and only then, did the little black hen look down. The fifth little chicken was exactly as the farmer's wife had described him, and she hung her head with shame. But for all that, she did her best to take special care of her little Half-Chick. The trouble was, that that was not what little Half-Chick wanted at all. When she

clucked to her little ones to come and nestle under her wings for safety, they scuttled, cheeping obediently, beneath her soft feathers. But not Half-Chick. Not he. He would be off, on his one leg, hoppitty-skip, hoppitty-skip, exploring the farm-yard, or at a safe distance, crowing defiance at the other young cockerels, so that the little black hen's comb grew quite pale with anxiety.

One fine day, Half-Chick said: 'I am sick and tired of this dull old farm-yard. And what is there to find in the field that I have not seen already? Today, I have decided I am going to Madrid, to see the King!'

'Cock-a-doodle-*don't*!' crowed the rooster. 'Cock-a-doodle-*don't*!'

But Half-Chick took not a bit of notice.

'Come back! Come back!' clucked the little black hen.

But still Half-Chick took not a bit of notice, for he was already half-way across the field. He didn't even wait to say good-bye.

On he went, with his beak in the air, more perky than ever, hoppitty-skip, hoppitty-skip, only pausing to steal a few grains of maize, or one or two beans, as he went by.

Presently he came to a stream, which was nearly choked with weeds and water-plants, so that its flow had become a mere trickle.

'Half-Chick! Little Half-Chick!' called the

Stream. 'Help! Please help me! I can scarcely move for the weeds that clog my bed! Will you not clear some of them away with your strong yellow beak?'

'Stop and help you?' said Half-Chick. 'No indeed! I've no time to spare, for I'm off to Madrid to see the King. He will be so pleased to see me that no doubt he will build me a silver hen-house!'

And on he went, skippitty-hop, skippitty-hop, without a thought for the poor Stream.

Next he came to a clearing in a wood, and there he found the remains of a fire, left behind by a wandering gypsy. Only a few embers were still glowing among the grey ash. The Fire cried out: 'Half-Chick! Little Half-Chick! Please help me! If you will only collect a few dry twigs, just one or two, and put them among my glowing embers so that my flames will dart up again, I shall not go out.'

'Stop and help you?' cried Half-Chick. 'No indeed! I've no time to spare. I am off to Madrid to see the King. He will be so pleased to see me that he will build me a silver hen-house, and I shall drink from a golden bowl.' And on he went, skippitty-hop, skippitty-hop, without another thought for the Fire.

When the sun set, he perched himself in the branches of a tree, and in the morning, when he woke, he heard the Wind moaning in its branches.

'Half-Chick! Little Half-Chick!' sighed the Wind. 'I don't know quite how it has happened, but I seem to have got myself tangled in these branches! Won't you help to set me free?'

'Stop and help you?' cried Half-Chick. 'No indeed! I've no time to spare, for I am off to Madrid to see the King. He will be so pleased to see me that he will build me a hen-house of silver, with a golden bowl to drink from, and I shall not be surprised if the Queen herself does not come and scatter my corn.' And so he went on, skippitty-hop, skippitty-hop, with his beak in the air, and not another thought for the Wind.

He hopped so far and so fast that quite soon he reached Madrid. Through the busy streets he went, skippitty-hop, skippitty-hop, until he came to the Palace. Now the King himself had just ridden through the Palace gate, and the sentries were still presenting arms as Half-Chick hopped through, bowing graciously to left and right as he did so.

'If the King's own soldiers present arms when I go by, it shows what an important person I must be, and how wise I was to leave the dull old farm-yard. Just wait until I meet the King himself!'

Unfortunately, it was not the King he met as

61

he went, skippitty-hop, skippitty-hop, across the courtyard, but the Palace Cook, with a basket on his arm. As neither of them was looking where he was going, they were equally surprised when the Cook stumbled over Half-Chick.

'Good gracious me, a chicken!' said the Cook. 'The very thing I want! Now I need not go to the market after all. For the King has ordered chicken soup for dinner, and there isn't a single bird in the royal hen-yard.'

As he spoke, he scooped up Half-Chick, and put him in his basket, and closed the lid on top of him with a snap. When he reached the kitchen he filled the soup-pot full of water and put it on the fire to boil. Then he dropped Half-Chick, plop, into the water, followed by a handful of carrots and onions and turnips. Half-Chick floundered about until he managed to get his head above the fast-warming water.

'Water! Water!' he cried. 'Help! Help! You are drowning me!'

But the Water only said: 'Aha! My young Half-Chick! You wouldn't help me when I asked you to clear some of the weeds from my stream. Even if I could, why should I help you now?'

Presently, Half-Chick cried: 'Fire! Fire! Help! Help! The pot is getting uncomfortably hot! You are burning me!'

'Aha! My young Half-Chick! You wouldn't

help me when I asked you to put some twigs on my few glowing embers. Even if I could, why should I help you now?'

Just as Little Half-Chick began to feel that he could not bear the heat any longer, the Cook lifted the lid of the pot, meaning to add a handful of salt to the soup, when he caught sight of Half-Chick.

'Good gracious me!' he cried, 'what is this miserable little half-a-chicken doing floating in the soup? That will never do to set before the King!'

And with his wooden spoon he scooped up Half-Chick and flung him through the door, where the Wind caught him up and whirled him away.

'Wind! Wind!' cried Little Half-Chick. 'Help me, please help! Put me down on the ground, for you whirl so fast that it takes my breath away!'

'Aha! My little Half-Chick!' said the Wind. 'You would not help me when I was tangled in the tree, why should I help you now? I shall teach you a lesson you will never forget.'

And the Wind whirled Little Half-Chick away and away, faster and faster over the city of Madrid; up and up he went until they reached the top of the tallest church.

And there the Wind left him, fixed to the very tip of the steeple. There you will find him to this day, standing on his one leg, looking over the city with his one eye. But now he does whatever the Wind commands. If it says 'Look north!' or 'Now look south!', that is exactly what he does.

No longer do the people of Madrid call him Half-Chick, but . . . a *Weathercock*!

(*From Spain*)

The Jackdaw's Skull

There was once a Chieftain who lived in the Hebrides. He had a young wife, and a baby son called Shamus, as bonny a baby as you could find in all the land.

'How quickly the wee bairn grows!' said his mother one day, as she and her husband sat talking of the brave and clever things they hoped he would do when he grew to be a man. 'See how he struggles already to sit up by himself! You know, I have been thinking: there is a saying among my people that when a babe is done with his mother's milk, if the first cup he drinks from is made from the skull of the jackdaw, he will grow up to have strange magical powers. I wonder if it might indeed be so?'

Her husband thought this no more than an old wive's tale, but to please his young wife, he brought her a jackdaw's skull. Bleached clean and white it was, from lying on the hillside in sun and rain, and more delicate than the finest china. And the baby drank from the strange cup, barely spilling a drop. When he had finished, his mother watched him anxiously, half-expecting some strange transformation to take place at once. But all he did was to put his thumb in his mouth and go fast asleep like any other baby.

And in time his parents forgot about the jackdaw's skull. And Shamus grew to be a sturdy young boy, who loved all outdoor sports and games, and who scrambled about in the heather with the other youngsters.

Now his mother had a linnet, which she kept in a wicker cage. She loved it for its red breast-feathers and its little twittering song. One day, she found the door of the cage open: the linnet was gone.

'How many times have I told you that if you open the cage to feed my bird, you must close the door carefully?' she said to Shamus.

'I opened it on purpose, to let the linnet go,' said Shamus. 'It asked me to, so piteously.'

'*Asked* you to?' said his mother angrily. 'You will be telling me next that you understand the language of birds!'

'But I do,' said Shamus simply. 'The linnet's pretty twittering told me how lonely he was in his prison, and how he longed to fly free with the other birds.'

And suddenly his mother remembered the jackdaw's skull, and scolded him no more.

Although in every other way Shamus seemed an ordinary boy, he would talk to the swallows that built their nests under the eaves, and they would tell him stories of their journeying over the sea, and of the warm distant lands where they spent the cold winter. He would help to settle the sparrows' quarrels, and in return they would tell him all the bird gossip.

As he grew older, he talked to the falcon on his wrist, the owl in the belfry, and the seagulls that followed, keening, over the newly-turned furrows behind the plough.

'That is good,' said his father. 'But more important still, he grows in strength and wisdom.'

Now, it had been the custom for many years, when the weather was cold and the mist covered the hills, for any bird that found its way into his father's great hall, to stay and share its warmth and comfort. They would perch high up on the smoky rafters and chatter sleepily to one another.

One evening, at supper, as Shamus waited on his father at the high table, as was usual, there was such a chatter and murmuration and whirring of wings high in the roof, that the Chieftain looked up and said: 'Tell me, my son, what is causing so much excitement among your feathered friends? What is it they are saying?'

Shamus shook his head. 'Do not ask me,' he replied. 'If I tell you, you will be angry.'

His father laughed and said: 'What nonsense is this? As if I could be angered by the chattering of a few birds! Tell the company what they say, I command you!'

'Very well,' said Shamus unhappily, 'I will tell you, though it is better that you should not know. They prophesy that the day will come when you, my father, shall wait upon *me* on bended knee, as I now wait on you this night.'

'What!' roared the Chieftain. 'You to become more important than your own father? So you plot to take my place? Never did I think my own son would grow up to be a traitor! Away with you out of my sight! Never will I set eyes on you again.'

It was in vain that Shamus explained, and his mother pleaded: it was no use. His father was too angry to listen. And so at last Shamus went sadly away, taking with him nothing but the clothes he stood up in.

He wandered down to the seashore. There he found a ship with her sails set and the tide on the turn.

'If I no longer have a home, I might do worse than go and see the world,' he said to himself. 'Perhaps there is some unskilled work that I could do on board the ship.'

The captain was quite willing to take on this strong-looking lad, for he was short of a ship's hand. And so Shamus set off on his travels. He made little money, but he saw many lands, and many strange people and customs, and became the wiser for it.

Some years later – and by this time he was a grown man – he grew tired of seafaring, and, leaving his ship at a bustling seaport, he set out on foot. He swung along the road, enjoying the firmness of dry land after the swaying of the ship's deck. Presently he came to a forest, which seemed to be all alive with wood-cutters. The sound of sawing, and chopping, and tumbling trees, was so loud that he was nearly deafened.

'Whose is this forest?' he yelled above the din to the nearest wood-cutter. 'And why are all the trees being cut down?'

'It belongs to the King,' the wood-cutter shouted back. 'We are felling the trees so that he can make a pleasure-garden beside the palace, for his new queen.'

On went Shamus, stumbling over fallen branches and tree-stumps, until he came to the edge of the forest. Now the palace was in sight, and the sound of tree-felling began to fade as he approached. But a different noise took its place. Everywhere he looked, there were birds, birds, birds. They flew in a clamouring cloud over the roofs and towers; they perched chattering on walls and window-ledges, weather-cocks and flag-poles; they sat on the helmets of the soldiers on guard – on their very halberds – and they chattered and cheeped and squawked and squeaked so that their noise was three times as loud as that of the wood-cutters.

'What is the meaning of this?' asked Shamus of one of the sentries, who was trying to prevent a couple of whistling starlings from perching on the muzzle of his musket.

'Can't you see and hear for yourself?' replied the soldier crossly, brushing a pair of blackbirds from his shoulders. 'A plague of birds! His Majesty is in despair. There seems to be no way of even keeping them out of the palace! Every door and window is locked and barred, but in they get somehow. The King and Queen can neither sleep nor talk to each other for their squawking. They say the birds even peck the food from the King's own plate. Thin as a spear-shaft he is growing with the worry of it.'

Shamus thought for a moment, and then he said: 'Perhaps I can help His Majesty, if you will take me to him.'

The King and Queen were sitting at breakfast. Birds perched upon the backs of every chair and on the top of every cupboard. They hopped about the table, chirruping and chattering. Round the rim of each plate sat a ring of birds, pecking at every mouthful as it was lifted on spoon or fork. It was no use the King asking the Queen why her tears splashed on to her plate, for she would not have heard him for the jabbering

of birds, any more than he would have heard her answer.

Shamus bowed low before the King, and making a trumpet of both his hands shouted into the royal ear: 'Your Majesty, I think I can help you in your distress.'

'Eh, what?' said the King. 'Speak up! I can't hear you!'

So Shamus shouted even louder: 'I think I can help you, because I speak the language of birds, and from what I have been able to hear in all this din, they feel that they are being ill-used.'

'*They* think *they* are being ill-used!' said the King. 'If you can help, then get on with it, do!' he went on, knocking a wren off the bread and butter he was about to put in his mouth. Then he added, more politely, 'If you can rid me of this plague of birds, I will give you whatever reward you ask.'

Shamus called out, in bird-language, 'Why do you persecute the King in this way?' For a moment there was an astonished silence. Then, there was such a deafening chattering and jumping up and down of birds that Shamus put his hands over his ears. 'Stop! Stop! One at a time, my friends!' he cried. 'Let the robin sitting on the rim of Her Majesty's cup tell me what is your trouble.'

Once more the birds fell silent, except for the robin, and in amazement the King and Queen listened to its excited twittering, and the strange language in which Shamus replied.

At last Shamus turned to the King and said, 'If Your Majesty will give orders that not one more tree shall be cut down, the birds will leave you in peace.'

'What is it to the birds what I do with my own trees?' said the King angrily.

'It has a great deal to do with them, sire,' said Shamus. 'Without trees their homes and their refuge are gone. They have nowhere to build their nests and lay their eggs. Already, half the forest is destroyed.'

The King sat frowning for a minute, and then he said: 'There is some truth in what you say. Kings and birds must defend their homes. I will give orders that no more trees are to be cut down.'

So the King summoned the wood-cutters, paid them well, and sent them on their way. And as the last man left with his axe over his shoulder, with a great whirring of wings a huge cloud of birds rose up into the air, circled the palace once, twice and again, before they flew away to the trees of the forest that still remained.

As soon as the King could bring himself to break the delicious silence that had fallen upon the palace, he said to Shamus, 'How can I reward you?'

And Shamus replied: 'There is only one thing I want. Give me a good ship, and men to sail her, so that I may return to my own country, for I long to see the misty hills of my own land again.'

And so he sailed away, and came once more to the Hebrides.

When he stepped ashore, the people ran to tell the Chieftain that a noble ship had anchored near by, and that the captain had already landed. (No one recognised the tall richly-dressed stranger as Shamus, who had left Scotland when he was not much more than a boy.)

'He is clearly some great man!' they said.

'Bring him to me with all speed,' said the Chieftain, 'that I may treat him with every honour.'

That night, Shamus sat at the high table in the great hall, and the Chieftain, on bended knee, offered him the cup of wine. Then Shamus could keep silent no longer.

'Father!' he said. 'Do you not recognise me? I am your son, Shamus. The prophecy of the birds has come true. You have waited on me just as I waited on you, all those years ago. But there is no more treachery in my heart today than there was then. Will you not take me back to serve you as your son once more?'

74

For a moment, the Chieftain looked at Shamus in astonishment. Then, he gave a great cry, and leaping up he embraced his son, and the rafters rang with the cheers of his people.

(*From the Hebrides*)

Why the Cock Crows

It is said in China that, long long ago, the Cock had horns. Shining silver horns they were, curving out on either side of his crimson comb. It is no wonder the hens bowed so humbly as he strutted by on his yellow legs. With his gleaming tail-feathers fluttering in the breeze he must have been a splendid sight. 'How handsome he is!' they clucked one to another.

One unlucky day, a dragon came to visit the Cock. (And although he too was handsome, with shining copper-coloured scales and green leathery wings, the hens did not stay to admire him. They ran away squawking in every direction, and watched from a safe distance.)

The Cock, however, held his ground, whatever he may have been feeling inside.

The Dragon landed, in a flurry of dust, and folded his great wings. The Cock noticed with relief that only a trickle of smoke rose from his red-rimmed nostrils. (When a dragon is feeling angry, or warlike, as everyone knows, he breathes fire, and showers of sparks.)

'Honourable singer of songs that delight the ear and ravish the soul, do things go well with you on this fine sunny morning?' said the Dragon.

'Well enough, honourable Dragon,' said the Cock cautiously. And, not to be outdone in politeness, he went on, 'May your scales ever outshine the brightness of the sun!'

'And do things go well with your many wives, who are as modest as no doubt they are beautiful?' went on the Dragon, licking his lips as he gave a sideways glance towards the circle of hens, who gazed at him warily with their bright eyes.

'They are well enough, I thank you,' replied the Cock, wondering what all this politeness was about.

There was a pause, while the Dragon made swirling patterns in the dust with his claw.

'And what brings you to my unworthy patch of ground?' asked the Cock, when he could hide his curiosity no longer.

The Dragon cleared his throat and said: 'I have a favour to ask of you. A very small favour,' he added hurriedly. 'I wish to go on a journey, to visit the Great Ones in the sky.'

'May your journey be swift and safe,' said the Cock. 'But what has that to do with me?'

'Only this,' said the Dragon. 'There is one

necessary thing I lack.' He paused again, and a few sparks flew up from his nostrils and fell with a sizzle in a small patch of mud. 'The fact is,' he went on at last, 'I want you to lend me your horns.'

'Lend you my horns!' exclaimed the Cock in astonishment. 'But why?'

'Because my dragon grandfather tells me it would be lacking in respect to the Great Ones to visit them without horns.'

'But how can this be?' said the Cock. 'There are many creatures who have no horns and feel it no disgrace. Even humans!'

'There you are wrong,' said the Dragon. 'Even humans are ashamed of their hornlessness. Why else do they cover their heads with those things they call hats, if not to hide their disgrace? I only ask to *borrow* your horns.'

'But how can I be sure you will return them?' said the Cock, who was a little alarmed to see that clouds of sparks were now soaring upwards in great puffs from the Dragon's nostrils.

'I shall return them by sunrise tomorrow,' said the Dragon.

'How do I know I can trust you?' said the Cock, greatly daring, for now a few flames flickered among the sparks.

The Dragon looked round thoughtfully, and at that moment a little pink worm popped its head up from a hole in the dusty ground.

'Aha!' said the Dragon, 'the very creature I wish to see! Greetings to you, honourable Worm! You and I are old friends, are we not?' (The Worm looked at the scaly claw which the Dragon was holding over his head, and he did not dare to say he had never seen the Dragon

79

before and hoped he never would again.) 'Will you set the mind of my friend Cock at rest, and assure him that I am a Dragon of my word?'

'Yes, yes, of course,' quavered the Worm, as the Dragon's scaly claw came even closer. 'His Mightiness the Dragon always keeps his promise.'

'Very well,' said the Cock, 'you may borrow my horns for this night only, but I must ask you as a favour to tell the Great Ones that the horns you wear are really mine.'

'It shall be as you ask,' said the Dragon, and there was now not a spark nor a flicker of flame to be seen coming from his nostrils. 'I shall return your horns tomorrow, by the time the sun rises.'

'How I wish I could come with you to visit the Great Ones in the sky,' said the Cock. 'But, alas, your wings are so much more powerful than mine that I should not be able to keep pace with you.'

And so the Cock lent the Dragon his silver horns. With a whirr of leather wings, the Dragon spiralled up into the blue sky, his copper scales glinting in the sunshine. As he went he called: 'Farewell! Till tomorrow at sunrise!'

The Cock and the Worm watched him go until he was a mere speck against the sun.

You may be sure, the next day they were there again, well before sunrise. But though they waited until the sun was high in the sky, there was no sign of the Dragon. They came again the next day, and the next, but there was still not a puff of smoke nor a copper scale of the Dragon to be seen, let alone the horns.

On the seventh morning the Cock lost all patience. He turned on the Worm and cried: 'Because you said the Dragon always kept his word, I let him borrow my beautiful silver horns. It is all your fault that I have lost them, perhaps for ever! What have you to say to that?'

But before the poor Worm had time to say a single word, or so much as wriggle, the Cock seized him with his sharp beak and swallowed him whole.

And that is why cocks have no horns, and why they all eat every worm they can see, and why each morning they lift their yellow bills to the rising sun and crow: 'Give us back the silver horns!'

(From the Chinese)

The Curse of the Black Knight

Have you ever seen a heron, standing as still as a sentinel on his long legs, in the shallow water on the edge of a river? With his slender neck lowered between hunched shoulders, he is clearly waiting for something — but what? Most people will tell you that he is keeping watch for fish. But in the River Elwy, in North Wales, there was once a Heron who was waiting for some*one*, not some*thing*.

It happened like this. Long long ago, one spring evening, when the willows were hanging out their catkins, and the hedgerows were starred with primroses, this heron was standing in the river, minding his own business — which meant snapping up a small fish now and then with his long bill — when a company of young men and maidens came riding by. The setting sun shone on their bright clothes, and their chatter and laughter was as merry as a flock of sparrows, the heron thought.

As they passed, one of the maidens reined in

her horse, and stood for a moment looking at the sunset light gleaming on the river, and her beauty outshone her companions as a linnet does a flock of crows. She paused for only a moment, but it was long enough for the Heron to fall head over heels in love.

As he watched her turn and ride away, he heard two frogs talking in the reeds behind him.

'So *that's* the daughter of the Prince of Derwyn' croaked one of them.

'So it is,' croaked the other. 'The Lady Myfanwy. Poor silly thing! She and her father the Prince have no more sense than a couple of tadpoles! There they are, both going cheerfully about their business, as though the curse of the Black Knight was not on them, when the Castle of Pengwern will come tumbling about their ears.'

'Ah! Squashed they will be in the ruins, like an ant when it's trod on,' went on the first frog. 'But what are humans to the likes of us? Still, I mustn't sit gossiping here. Good day to you, my friend!' And he jumped into the river with a 'plop'.

But before his companion could follow, quick as lightning the heron stabbed with his great bill, and caught him by the hind leg.

'What is this talk of the Lady Myfanwy? And curses? And tumbling castles?' he hissed. (It is not easy to talk clearly while holding a frog in your beak.) 'Speak, or I shall eat you up!'

'Mercy! Mercy, Sir Heron!' said the frog, with a muffled croak. (It is not easy to speak clearly when you are held upside down by a heron.) 'Spare my life, and I will tell you all I know!'

So the heron put the trembling frog on a stone, keeping his long yellow bill ready poised, in case he should try to escape.

'I wonder you haven't heard about it already,' quavered the frog. 'But living so high up in the air as you do, perhaps you don't hear all the gossip?' And he cocked a bulging eye up at the heron.

'Go on! Go on!' snapped the heron impatiently. And the frog went on hurriedly. 'They say that when the Prince of Derwyn clapped the wicked Black Knight into the deepest dungeon of his castle, because of his evil ways, the scoundrel knight discovered a great crack in a corner of the dungeon floor. And when he escaped, he cursed the Prince of Derwyn and the Lady Myfanwy, and vowed to destroy them. Ever since then, he has bribed and bullied the rats he fed while he was captive, to gnaw and nibble at the foundations of the castle, so that the crack is growing wider and wider.'

'What then?' said the heron.

'Why, the crack has become a great gaping

hole, and at the spring tide, when the moon rises, the sea will come swirling through, and the castle will come crashing down on the Lady Myfanwy and the Prince, and every living thing within!'

'Is it possible that there can be such wickedness?' said the heron. 'But how can I warn them of their danger, when I only speak the language of birds and beasts?'

The frog thought for a minute, and then he said: 'They do say that there is a fish living in the moat of the castle, who speaks the human tongue. If you were to catch him with your great beak, perhaps you could persuade *him* to tell the Prince instead?'

'But how shall I know this wonderful fish among so many?' said the heron.

'That is easy,' replied the frog. 'They say he has only one eye.'

'Then there is no time to lose, for the spring tide is in three days' time!' said the heron. And, with a swish of his grey wings, and a clatter of his bill, he sailed up into the air.

Now, as the heron stood in the castle moat, waiting for the one-eyed fish, who should come picking rushes by the water but the Lady Myfanwy! When she saw the heron, she stopped, and exclaimed: 'Where do you come from, you beautiful bird? Never before have I seen a heron standing in the castle moat!'

Of course, the heron could not answer, but he lifted his crest, and bowed his slender neck in homage, and fell even more madly in love with her than before. So love-lorn was he, that he quite forgot about catching the one-eyed fish. Instead, he filled his time with mooning after his lady-love, and gazing round for a further glimpse of her.

For two days he gazed and gawped about, but on the morning of the third day, who should come – not the Lady Myfanwy – but the castle cook, with two of the scullions. They sat themselves down by the side of the moat and began to fish, and as they fished, they gossiped about the great feast that was to be held that night in the castle, when the Prince came home from hunting. And *still* the heron thought of nothing but the beauty of the Lady Myfanwy.

'Now, don't forget,' said the Cook to the scullions, 'that none but the finest fish will do for the feast. Anything else, you can throw back into the water.'

The heron was just going to move away from the sound of their chatter, when one of the scullions caught a fish. Suddenly, he shouted with laughter.

'What's the joke?' asked his companions.

'Why, this fish is the joke! It's only got one eye! I never saw a one-eyed fish before!'

And *then* the heron remembered.

'Two precious days I have wasted, mooning after the Lady Myfanwy, instead of trying to catch the fish that speaks the human tongue!' he said to himself. 'And now it has been caught by a scullion, and will be fried and eaten before I can ask it to warn the Prince of his terrible danger. For this is the third day, and the spring tide is at moonrise this very night!' And he hung his head in shame. But not for long; for suddenly he heard the cook say: 'A poor one-eyed fish will never do for the feast: throw it back in the moat again!'

'It may be no good for the Prince,' said the scullion, with a laugh. 'Maybe it will do for a heron!'

And as the silver fish came flashing through the air, the heron caught it with his great yellow bill.

'Mercy! Mercy! Sir heron!' cried the fish.

'You have nothing to fear from me,' said the bird. 'You have but to promise you will repeat to the Prince of Derwyn exactly what I shall tell you, and then you may go free once more.'

You may be sure that the one-eyed fish agreed to this. 'But how shall we reach the Prince?' he asked, when he had heard what he had to say. 'Even so grand a bird as you would not be allowed inside the castle.'

'When we hear the trumpets blow, we shall

know that the Prince is back from hunting, and that the feast has begun,' replied the heron. 'And in a little while no one will have eyes or ears for anything but the merrymaking in the Great Hall. Once inside we must trust to luck.'

And so they waited, and when darkness came the heron marched up to the castle, with the one-eyed fish in his beak.

He knocked with his bill on the castle gate.

'Who is there?' called the soldier on guard.

'A latecomer to the Prince's feast,' said the one-eyed fish. And as soon as the gate was open, the heron slipped inside, unnoticed by the soldier, whom they left peering into the darkness. Not until they reached the door of the Great Hall itself were they challenged again.

'What have we here?' said the soldier on guard. 'If it isn't a bird, with a smelly great fish in its beak!' He was just reaching for his sword, when who should come by but the Lady Myfanwy.

'Why, if it isn't the handsome heron who has been standing in the moat these three days past! Put up your sword, soldier.'

'But the fish, lady . . .?'

The Lady Myfanwy laughed. 'No doubt a gift for the Prince, my father. Follow me, Sir Heron! It will amuse the company.'

The heron bowed his long neck in homage, and the Lady laughed again and dropped him a

curtsey, and as they made their stately progress
through the hall, the company fell silent. Only
the harpist went on playing. When they reached
the High Table, the Lady Myfanwy said: 'One of
your loyal subjects has brought a gift for the
Prince of Derwyn!'

As she spoke, the heron placed the one-eyed
fish on the golden plate which lay before the
Prince.

'My thanks,' began the Prince, with a laugh. 'It
shall be baked in butter and herbs and –'

But to his astonishment the fish interrupted. 'I come not to be eaten, but to warn you, Prince!'

And the company was so astounded to hear a fish talk that you could have heard a feather fall.

He told of the curse of the wicked Black Knight; of the rats, gnawing and nibbling at the foundations of the castle; and how, at moonrise that very night, the sea would come bursting through, swishing and swirling, higher and higher, till the castle rocked and came crashing down upon every living thing within.

As he finished speaking, the Prince of Derwyn sprang to his feet.

The dark sky was growing lighter.

'The moon is rising even now! Save yourselves, my people, while you can!'

As he spoke, far below they could hear a mighty rumbling, and with that, the gallant company rose up, and with shouts and cries rushed from the Great Hall, till the Prince, the Lady Myfanwy, the heron and the one-eyed fish were left alone. And now they could hear the sound of rushing water.

'Make haste!' said the fish, as the rumbling grew louder and the floor began to rock. 'Follow our friend the heron!' And as they hurried away, the light of the full moon flooded through the windows of the Great Hall.

So the good heron led them to safety through the rising waters, just in time, for as they reached the other side of the moat, there was a deafening crash, and the castle fell in ruins behind them.

Then the heron led them, by quick and secret ways, to the river, where a small boat was moored. The Prince of Derwyn and the Lady Myfanwy climbed aboard, and as he cast off, the Prince cried: 'My undying gratitude to you, Sir Heron, and to you, my one-eyed fish! You shall have your reward when we return!'

And as he rowed away, the Lady Myfanwy called: 'As we go by the river, so shall we come back. Until then, farewell!'

And that is why the Heron waited; and for all I know he is waiting still.

(From Wales)

Comatas and the Bees

Long, long ago, when the world was young, and the people who lived in Greece said their prayers to the god Zeus, there was a young man called Comatas, who minded his master's goats on the slopes of Mount Helicon. He led a carefree life, with the goats for company, for he loved them dearly, and took great care that no wild animal should harm them. He lived on roots, wild berries and goat's milk, and when the sun was hot he sat in the shade of the trees and played on his pipes. And very sweetly he played too. He liked to think that the goats listened, and when they bounded up and down that they were dancing to his music.

Now the goats were not the only creatures to listen to his piping. The nymphs, the spirits who lived in the trees and streams, and who were seldom seen by men, often slipped between the tree trunks and stood where the shadow of the leaves was darkest, to hear his merry playing.

'It is a strange thing,' said Comatas to his goats

one day, 'but sometimes I seem to see a lock of hair stir in the breeze beneath the trees, and when I look again, it is nothing but a hanging creeper. Sometimes a lovely face seems to smile at me from among the bushes, yet, when I look again, there is no one there.'

The goats gazed at him with their strange yellow eyes, and then kicked up their heels and scampered off together, as though they shared a joke they could not tell him.

One summer night, when the moon was full, Comatas woke to hear distant music and sweet singing. Rising to his feet, he followed the sound, which led him to a clearing in the forest. There, in the pale light, he saw the slender figures of the nymphs dancing round three stately figures, and singing as they danced. Behind them, by a little stream, was an altar.

'These must be very important people,' said Comatas to himself. 'Perhaps they are the gods who watch over the slopes of the mountain, and who make the trees so shady, and the grass so sweet for my goats to feed upon. How I wish I could give them something to show how grateful I am! But what has a poor goat-herd to give?'

He watched, until the moon set, and the dancing ceased, and the figures seemed to melt into the trees. He rubbed his eyes. Had he dreamed it all? He was sure he had not.

'I shall play them the gayest tunes I can think of; and why should I not give them one of the finest kids of my flock?'

So that was what he did. He played on his pipes till the goats could scarcely keep still; and the finest kid of the whole number he left upon the little altar in the clearing in the forest.

Now, Comatas had lived so long with his goats on the mountainside that he had quite forgotten that they were not his to give. When he drove them down the mountain to the courtyard of his master, and the flock was counted, one animal was missing. His master, who was a hard man, was very angry indeed.

'You are nothing better than a thief!' he

shouted. 'What have you done with one of my valuable goats?' And before Comatas could explain, he struck him, so hard that he fell sprawling on the ground. Then he ordered his slaves to pick him up and put him in a great wooden chest which stood by the door.

'And there you shall stay, to think about your wickedness, until I choose to let you go!' he said, as he turned the great key in the lock, and put it in his pocket.

It was not long before the nymphs missed the cheerful sound of the goat-herd's pipe. 'Where can he be?' they asked one another.

'We must send someone to search for him,' said the chief among them, and she caught a little grey moth, and sat it on her finger. 'Go and search till you find what has become of Comatas the goat-herd, and then come back and tell me.'

The moth fluttered away on silent wings. At last it came to the house of the cruel master. Having flown a long way, and feeling quite worn out, it perched on a great wooden chest, so that it might fan itself for a little with its wings. Suddenly, it heard a movement inside the chest. Now, a great big key has to have a great big keyhole. So the moth fluttered down, and peered through with its bright eyes, and inside it saw Comatas, who told it all that had happened.

When the nymphs heard the story they said:

'Surely he will die if he is left long in that great chest without food?' And they put their heads together, and made a plan.

That very day, buzzing busily, a bee flew through the keyhole into the chest. With him he carried his sack of honey, and out he came without it. He was followed by another bee, and another, and another, until a stream of them buzzed their way through the keyhole. And so it went on day after day.

Several weeks later, the master of Comatas said to himself: 'By now my thieving goat-herd must have paid the price of his dishonesty.' And, taking the great key out of his pocket, he fitted it into the lock of the chest, expecting to find Comatas lying dead inside. But what was his surprise, when he lifted the lid and out sprang the goat-herd, as fit and merry as the day he had been imprisoned!

When Comatas explained how every day the good little bees had fed him with their honey, building honeycombs in the chest, and how they had cheered him with their buzzing, his master changed his tune, and ever after treated Comatas with great respect, for he knew that the wild bees were under the special protection of the great god Zeus himself.

(*From Greece*)

Prince Michael and the Swan Maid

Once upon a time there was a Tsar of Russia whose only son grew tired of leading the life of a young prince.

'I must always do this, because I am the son of the Tsar, and I must not do that, because I am the son of the Tsar. I must wear heavy uncomfortable clothes, and spend my time being polite to boring people, and all because I am the son of the Tsar!' he said to himself.

One day, he decided to run away and seek his fortune like any other young man. He slipped out of the Palace early one morning. No one recognised the youth with tousled hair, wearing a plain cloak, as young Prince Michael. For did not the Tsar's son dress in scarlet and gold, with a hairdresser to arrange his dark curls every morning?

Sometimes he walked and sometimes he ran. On and on he went, until he found himself in a strange kingdom. He began to grow very hungry. As the son of the Tsar, he had never had to think of where the next meal was coming from. Delicious food just seemed to happen at the right moment. But now, he had to manage as best he could with nuts and berries, and very tired of them he grew.

'There is no doubt about it,' he said to himself, as he walked one day through a wood. 'I must earn some money to buy food. I am so hungry I would work for a week for nothing but a loaf of bread and a hunk of cheese.'

As he tightened his belt to its last hole, he came to a clearing in the wood in which was a tumbledown hut. By the door, from which came a wonderful smell of rabbit stew, stood a strange old man. His long white hair grew down to his waist, and his beard was long enough to keep his knees warm.

'Work?' said the old man in reply to the Prince's question. 'I can give you plenty of that, but I have no money to give you. However, if you will work for me for three years, I will feed you well, and give you a bed to sleep in. If, at the end of this time, you have served me faithfully, then I promise you as your reward a beautiful wife. What do you say to that?'

Well, Prince Michael was so hungry, and the smell of rabbit stew was so bewitching, that he said, 'Done!' (He hardly gave a thought to the beautiful wife who was to be his at the end.)

For three years he worked, and when the three years were nearly up the old man said, 'Today you shall neither cut wood nor draw water. Instead, you must go to the lake at the end of the wood, walk round it three times, cracking the whip I shall give you as you go. Then come back and tell me exactly what you have seen.'

Prince Michael did as he was told, though it seemed a foolish way of spending a sunny day.

'Well, what did you see?' asked the old man when he returned.

'Why, nothing but a few fish leaping from the water, and the sunlight shining on the ripples,' said the Prince.

'Then do the same thing again tomorrow,' said the old man.

'And what did you see this time?' he asked next day.

'Why, a wonderful sight!' said the Prince. 'As I walked round the lake for the third time, a flock of swans came gliding down. As soon as they landed by the water, they took off their white robes and became beautiful girls! They bathed in the lake, then they put on their white robes once more and became swans, and flew off towards the sunset with a great beating of wings.'

The old man nodded as though this was just what he expected.

'Tomorrow,' he said, 'you must do the same thing for the third time. But while the Swan Maids are bathing, snatch up their white robes, and bring them back to me.'

Next day, while the Swan Maids swam in the lake, Prince Michael gathered up their soft white robes and took them back to the hut.

'But what will they do without them?' he asked the old man. Before he had time to answer, there was the sound of bare feet running, and the Swan Maids came flocking into the clearing.

'Give us back our white robes!' they begged in distress, 'for without them we must stay humans for ever!'

'Why, willingly, my dears!' said the old man, bowing so deeply that his white beard swept the ground. One by one he gave them back their white robes, and one by one they flew away. But when he came to the last girl, who was the most beautiful of them all, he turned to the Prince and said: 'You have worked faithfully and well for three years. Did I not promise you a beautiful wife? Well, here she is. Take the white robe and keep it safe. Never, never let her wear it again.'

Prince Michael turned to the girl, who was indeed the loveliest he had ever seen, and said, 'Will you be my wife?'

The Swan Maid lifted her drooping head. 'I have no choice,' she said.

And so they were married.

As it was long since he had seen his parents, the Prince decided after all to go home to the court of the Tsar. And on the way the girl grew to love her young husband. His royal parents welcomed them both with open arms.

Now, Prince Michael had given the white robe to his mother, the Tsarina. 'Put it safely away,' he said to her, 'and be sure never to let my wife wear it. I leave it in your charge.'

The Swan Maid was happy in her new life, but as time went by she began to long to fly just once more with her sisters in the freedom of the air. So one day she said, 'Dear Mother, will you not let me try on the white robe to see if it still fits?'

Remembering her son's warning, the Tsarina shook her head.

A few days later, the Swan Maid tried again. But still the answer was, 'No'.

When she asked a third time, the Tsarina grew a little flustered, for she could think of no good excuse for refusing so natural a request.

'To tell the truth, my dear,' she said at last, 'I – I I . . . er . . . have forgotten where I put it –' (which was certainly *not* the truth) – 'I am sure I have put it somewhere safe.'

'If that is all,' said the Swan Maid to herself, 'I shall just have to find it for myself.'

So one morning when the Tsarina was asleep, in the heat of the day, she searched her chests and her closets until at last she found the white robe.

'Look, mother dear, I have found it!' she cried. And the Tsarina woke to see her slip it over her head, and at once become a white swan again.

'Tell my dear husband,' cried the swan, as it rose in the air on wide white wings, 'tell him to search for me at the top of the Glass Mountain!'

And with that, she flew through the window, and the beat of her wings grew fainter and fainter until it faded into silence.

The Prince was overcome with sorrow when he heard his mother's story.

'The Glass Mountain?' he said. 'Where is that? How can I find it?'

The Tsar had no idea, neither had the wisest men in his kingdom. At last a very old man said: 'The greatest travellers in the world are the four winds. There is no corner of the earth they do not know. Ask them where the Glass Mountain is.'

The Tsar asked the East Wind, and the West Wind, and the South Wind, and they could none of them tell him the answer. But the North Wind said: 'It is on the other side of the world. I will help your son to the Glass Mountain.'

So the North Wind took a deep breath – so

deep that his cheeks nearly cracked – and with a mighty swoosh! sent the young Prince spinning away and away, until he landed at the foot of the Glass Mountain.

He looked up at its jagged sloping sides, and was nearly blinded by the light that glanced from a hundred points and pinnacles. However, he lowered his eyes and began to climb. But as fast as he climbed a little way he slithered down again. At last he took off his shoes and tried once more, and though he often slipped, he began to make progress.

Up and up he struggled, until he reached the very top. There he found a cave, and in it sat an old witch-woman, spinning a fine thread of glass at her spinning-wheel.

She cackled with laughter when she heard the young man's story.

'I have three hundred Swan Maidens, all exactly alike, who will come when I summon them,' said the old witch. 'You can try to find your wife among them if you wish. But if you fail, you must stay a prisoner in my glass cave, to do my will for ever and ever.'

'And if I succeed?' said the Prince.

'Then you may take her away. At the foot of the Mountain there is a herd of horses. Choose which you like to carry you home.'

The old woman rose from her spinning-wheel, and taking a horn which was hanging on the wall, she blew a deafening blast, which echoed from all the hills around. And presently, faint at first, but growing louder and louder, came the sound of the beating of wings, and a great string of snow-white swans flew towards them. As each one landed outside the cave, it turned into a beautiful girl, and each one of them was as exactly like the next as a pin is exactly like another pin.

'Well, why don't you choose?' asked the old

witch. 'Is it this one?' – pointing with a bony finger. The Prince shook his head. 'Or this?' But every time, with anxiety growing in his heart, Prince Michael said: 'No, that is not my wife.'

At last they came to the two hundred and ninety ninth Swan Maid, and the old witch cackled so loud and so long she might have been laying an egg. In despair, the Prince shook his head again. But when the old woman pointed to the three hundredth beautiful girl, the girl gave him a wink. Just the faintest flutter of an eyelid.

'*This* is my wife!' said Prince Michael, and he took her in his arms, to the great joy of them both.

You may be sure the old witch stopped cackling at this. Instead, she ground her teeth in fury (the only two teeth she had), for she had been sure of keeping the young man as her servant in the Glass Cave.

'Tricked!' she cried. 'Tricked! Get out of my sight the pair of you!' Which of course they were only too glad to do.

Hand in hand they slipped and slithered down the Glass Mountain, half a hundred times more quickly than the Prince had climbed up.

At the foot of the mountain, as the witch had promised, they found a herd of horses grazing, tall and strong, with arched necks and flowing manes.

'Do as I say,' said the Swan Maid. 'Take the meanest and ugliest horse of them all.'

So the Prince chose a poor spavined creature, with staring coat and lack-lustre eyes. But no sooner had he leapt upon its back, with the Swan Maid before him, than the horse lifted its head proudly, its coat became bright and silky, and from its shoulders grew a pair of splendid wings.

And Prince Michael and the Swan Maid flew back to the court of the Tsar in triumph, and they both lived happily ever after.

(From Russia)

The Good Hunter

There was once a mighty hunter of the Red Indian tribe of the Iroquois. Strange though it may seem, although he was a hunter he was dearly loved by all the animals, for he hunted for food alone, and would feed and tend all wounded creatures, both great and small.

Now there was a bitter feud between the Iroquois and a neighbouring tribe. In a fierce battle, which lasted from sunrise until the shadows lengthened in the evening, many braves were killed.

It was the Fox who found the body of the Hunter on the field of battle. When he saw that his scalp had been taken by his enemies, and that there was no life in him, he sat on his haunches and raising his muzzle to the rising moon sang a dirge, a sad solemn lament in memory of the friend of all the animals. Then, still singing his dirge, he trotted off to spread the news.

The first animal he met was the Bear.

'Our friend the Hunter slain?' said the Bear.

'Let us call a council of the animals so that we may discuss what can be done.'

And so all the animals came together: the deer, the elk, the marten, the moose, the mink and the caribou, with every other creature that leaps and runs.

The sun was rising by the time they had all assembled.

'Our friend, the Good Hunter,' said the Bear. 'He who has fed and tended us, has been killed in battle and his scalp taken. Is there anyone among you who can think of a way to bring him back to life?'

There was a stirring among the animals as they whispered together, but not one of them answered.

'Can no one think of anything?' went on the Bear. 'Alas! Alas!' And he threw up his great muzzle, and he too began to sing a dirge.

One by one the other animals joined in, until their sad song grew so loud that it was heard, miles away, by the Golden Oriole.

'By my black and golden feathers,' said the Oriole, 'I have never heard such a loud and mournful sound before! I must fly as fast as I am able and find out what terrible thing has happened.'

As he flew, he was joined by all the other birds, and they swept in a great cloud towards the sound of the distant singing.

When they reached the council of the animals, who were rocking from side to side in their sorrow, the Oriole said to the Bear: 'What has happened to make all the animals sing so sadly and so loud that it can be heard from miles away?'

'Our good friend the Hunter is dead,' moaned the Bear, 'and his scalp taken by his enemies.'

'That is sad news indeed,' said the Oriole. 'For he was a friend to birds as well as beasts. But instead of making all this noise, why do you not *do* something?'

'What is there to do?' said the Bear sorrowfully.

'The first thing,' said the Oriole, 'is to discover

the camping ground of his enemies, and there we shall find his scalp, without which no man can live.'

All the birds and beasts clamoured to be allowed to go in search of the Good Hunter's enemies, but – 'Peace! Peace!' cried the Oriole. 'This thing can only be done by stealth and cunning.'

'No one can move with more stealth and cunning than I,' said the Fox. 'After all, it was I who found our friend the Hunter. Let me go!'

So the Fox set out. He searched here and he searched there, but he could find no sign of the Hunter's enemies. At last, after several days, footsore and weary, he came back to the council, no wiser than when he started.

Then the Hawk said: 'I, who fly so swiftly and so high in the air, I shall see the smoke of their fires from far away. Let me go next!'

So off flew the Hawk, and though he saw smoke rising in the distance from many fires, he flew over each camp so fast and so high that he could see nothing so small as a scalp.

'Now, I fly slowly and with great dignity,' said the Heron, when the Hawk returned. 'I shall be able to see all that goes on below me. Let me go next!'

So the Heron flew off with slow strokes of his powerful wings. But he had not gone far before

110

he saw some vines below him, hung with many ripe beans.

'Surely I can stop for a few minutes to eat a few beans?' he said to himself. But so delicious were the beans, and he ate so many of them, that he became so heavy he could not fly any longer.

When the Heron did not return, the Raven said: 'I do not fly fast or high, but all men are so used to seeing me that I may hop about where I choose, and no one will notice me. I will go next.'

And so the Raven flew away, and circling low over the first camp he came to, he landed in the middle of the Meeting Place, and no one took any notice of him at all as he hopped about. And then at last he saw what he was looking for. The Good Hunter's scalp was hanging, for all to see, on a wooden post. The Raven waited till it grew dusk, and then he seized the scalp, and flew away with it in triumph.

When he reached the council, instead of praising him, the Bear shook his head. 'What use is this dried-up withered thing that has been hanging in the sun? How can it be fitted on to anyone's head?'

Then the Great Eagle said: 'As I sit upon my nest above the clouds, the dew collects on my back between my wings. Could we not use this to soften it?'

And so the scalp was made soft and supple in the dew.

Then the Bear said: 'But what shall we stick it on with?'

Now the Good Spirit had watched, and seen how the birds and the animals had worked together to bring the Hunter back to life, and he was pleased. And he put it into the heads of the birds that they should collect certain leaves and pieces of bark, and soak them in dew, which became sticky as any glue. Then, led by the Fox, the birds and the animals set off to where the dead Hunter lay.

Smeared with the glue, the scalp fitted his head as though it had never been taken away. It was not even possible to see the join.

No sooner had this been done, than the Good Hunter opened his eyes and sat up. He stretched himself and gave a great yawn. 'What a refreshing sleep I have had!' he said. 'But how glad I am to be awake again. I dreamed that I was surrounded by a great host of my friends the birds and animals. A great host. . .'

But when he looked round, there was not one to be seen, for as soon as he opened his eyes they had all tiptoed away.

(*From North America*)

The Word of Power

There was once a Caliph of Baghdad, who was young, rich and wise, but not quite wise enough, for he had made an enemy of the powerful Wizard Kaschnur, and it is not wise to offend those who deal in magic.

One day, the Caliph sat at his ease on a pile of silken cushions, smoking his hubble-bubble, and fanned by a beautiful slave, when his thoughts were interrupted by the sound of chatter and laughter outside in the court below. He clapped his hands and sent for his Grand Vizier.

'What is the cause of this clamour?' he demanded.

'It is nothing of any importance, My Lord,' said the Vizier, bowing low. 'Merely a travelling pedlar, who has things to sell the like of which I have never seen before, so beautiful are they.'

'Then let him be brought before me, so that I too may see them,' said the Caliph. And so the pedlar was summoned.

He was a squat, ugly, squint-eyed fellow, with

a straggling, greasy beard. He bowed so low before the Caliph that his forehead nearly touched the marble floor, but if he was ugly, the things he unpacked from his basket were of surprising beauty. There were necklaces and brooches of pearls and emeralds; there were jewelled rings and bracelets; and daggers with curiously carved handles; and carvings in coral, ivory and jade.

The Caliph bought several pretty things, and with many respectful bowings, the pedlar replaced the rest in his basket. He was just preparing to go when the Caliph said: 'Stay! There is something you have left behind. What is that small box on the floor behind you?'

The pedlar stooped and picked it up, saying as he did so: 'A thousand apologies, my lord! I have the memory of a squirrel and the impudence of a monkey to leave my rubbish on your honour's marble floor, for that is what it is. Merely something I found lying on the cobblestones of the market-place.'

The Caliph held out his hand for the little box. 'It is cleverly made,' he said. 'And the carving on the lid is curious.'

'Then will you not accept it as an unworthy present from a humble pedlar? – No, no, I will accept no money for it, my lord,' said the pedlar. 'It is enough that you have shown pleasure in my humble store. There is nothing inside the box but a little powder, and a scrap of parchment, with something scribbled on it which I cannot read.'

When the pedlar was gone, the Caliph opened the box. The powder inside was greenish, with a curious heady smell. Tucked into the lid was a small piece of parchment covered with closely crabbed writing. Neither the Caliph nor the Grand Vizier could make head nor tail of this.

'I am determined to find out what it means,' said the Caliph. 'Let the most learned men in the land be summoned! Who knows, someone may be found who can read this strange writing.'

And so the most learned men in the land came to the palace. They passed the parchment from hand to hand, and wagged their beards over it, and nodded their grey heads, for they all agreed at last that the writing was in Latin.

'What it says is this,' said the oldest and most learned of them all, bowing as low as his ancient back would let him. '"He who would understand the language of all living creatures, and would transform himself into any fish, fowl, or beast of his choice, must first snuff a pinch of the green powder, while crying out the name of the creature he wishes to become. He must then bow three times to the east, crying in a loud voice as he does so: 'Mutabor! Mutabor! Mutabor!' When he wishes to return to his human form once more, he must bow three times to the *west*, calling out the same word of power, 'Mutabor!' But woe betide him who laughs whilst wearing the shape of his chosen creature, for he will at once forget the magic word, and remain an animal for ever and ever."'

After swearing the learned men to secrecy, the Caliph rewarded them well and sent them away. Then, laughing heartily, he said to his Vizier: 'By the Beard of the Prophet, it is as well that the Pedlar could not read the parchment, for surely the box is beyond price! Tomorrow, at sunrise, let us go out into the country and try our luck with this magic powder.'

Next morning, as soon as the sun had risen, the

Caliph and the Vizier set out together, leaving their attendants behind. As they walked through the garden, they discussed what kind of animal each of them would choose to become.

'Not a toad, for example,' said the Caliph, who had seen one crouching beneath a dockleaf. 'Far too ugly!'

'Not a honey bee,' said the Grand Vizier, as one buzzed past. 'Too hard-working!'

Presently they reached the shores of a lake, on the banks of which a stork was strutting up and down on his long legs.

'Ah! Now, a stork!' said the Caliph. 'That is a creature of dignity that I should not scorn to be.'

'What can it be saying when it clatters its bill so loudly?' said the Vizier.

'Now is our chance to find out,' replied the Caliph. 'Luck is with us: there is another bird flying towards it. Let us change ourselves into storks, and hear what they have to say to one another. But for the love of Allah, let us remember not to laugh.'

So, at the self-same moment, each of them took a pinch of the green powder, and wished to become storks. Then, bowing low three times to the east, they cried, 'Mutabor! Mutabor! Mutabor!' And in the twinkling of an eye, storks they were, with long necks, long red beaks, and even longer thin red legs, their black feathers gleaming in the morning sun. They looked at one another in astonishment, but the sound of voices soon drew their attention. The bird they had first seen by the water's edge had been joined by the other.

'You are late, my beloved,' said the first stork. 'I have waited this long time fearing that something had happened to you. What was it that kept you from your own true love?'

'It was not my wish to keep you waiting, beloved,' said the second stork. 'But tonight my father has commanded me to dance before a company of his guests. So that I do not bring shame upon him, I had to stay and practise what I should do.'

'Alas, that I should not be there to see. Will you not show me how you will dance?'

Spell-bound, the Caliph and the Grand Vizier watched, while in time with the loud clattering of her bill in a kind of song the young stork pranced backwards and forwards on her long legs, hopping and sidling up and down. But when she stood swaying on one red leg while she waved the other high in the air, flapping her white wings and writhing with her long neck, they both burst out laughing, and the two storks flew away.

'That was the funniest thing I've ever seen!' said the Caliph, still shaking with laughter. But

the Grand Vizier stopped laughing suddenly.
'My Lord,' he said, 'we were warned that on no
account must we laugh! What was the word of
power that would turn you back to Caliph and
me to Grand Vizier again? It has quite gone from
my mind!'

'It began with M,' said the Caliph. 'That I do
remember. M . . . Mu . . . Mu . . . it is no use. I
have quite forgotten what it was.' And however
many times they bowed to the west, mumbling
'M . . . Mu . . . Mu . . .' they both remained
storks. At last they gave it up. 'Allah have mercy
on us!' said the Caliph. 'For storks we must
remain for ever.'

For some weeks they wandered unhappily

along the shore of the lake, living on frogs and small fish, until one day the Caliph said: 'I long to hear the sound of human voices again. Let us leave this desolate place and fly over the houses of Baghdad. There we can take refuge on the roof of the palace.'

But as they flew over the city, they heard the sound of a great crowd, cheering and shouting: 'Hail, mighty Mirza! Lord of Baghdad! Hail! Hail!'

'Now I understand it all,' said the Caliph as they circled overhead. 'This enchantment is the work of my enemy Kaschnur the Wizard, for Mirza is his son. There is no hope for us here.' And the two storks flew sorrowfully away.

They flew until their wings grew weary. 'I can fly no more,' said the Caliph at last. 'Night is drawing on. There seems to be a ruin below in which we may shelter for the night.'

The ruin showed signs of past splendour. Some of the walls and broken pillars still showed the remains of rich colours. They were about to make themselves as comfortable as they were able for the night, when the Vizier said: 'My Lord, this is an evil place! Do you not hear that sobbing sound, as of someone in torment?'

'Nonsense!' said the Caliph. 'It is nothing but the cry of an owl!'

Which is just what it turned out to be. They

found her moaning sadly, as owls will, in a small ruined chamber with a broken door. When she saw the two storks her hooting ceased and she greeted them joyfully.

'Who are you? And what are you doing in this unhappy place?' she asked softly. 'Are you too victims of the evil Wizard Kaschnur?'

The Caliph and the Vizier, who of course could now understand owl language, told her their story. 'But what brings you here?' went on the Caliph.

'Like you, I am the victim of that wicked man,' the Owl replied. 'Kaschnur demanded my hand in marriage for his hateful son Mirza, and my father, who is King of the Indies, had him thrown from the palace. But by means of a poisoned drink he turned me into the owl you see me, and carried me off to live in this dismal ruin, with nothing but rats and bats to keep me company. As I would not marry Mirza, here I must stay, until someone of his own free will asks me to be his bride.'

'Alas!' said the Vizier, 'I already have a wife.' But the Caliph said nothing, for though the owl was beautiful – for an owl – who could tell what she would be as a human?

'I may be able to help you,' the Owl went on. 'This very night, Kaschnur comes here to feast with his friends in an underground cavern. Often

121

they tell stories of their wicked doings. Perhaps you may hear something that may be useful to you. Follow me.'

On silent white wings the Owl circled the ruined room. Then she led the two storks down a dark underground passage. Soon, they heard the sounds of shouting and laughter, and peering through a hole in the broken wall, they saw a company of men sitting round a table covered with rich foods and flagons of wine.

'There is Kaschnur himself!' said the Caliph.

'And beside him sits the Pedlar who gave you the carved box with the green powder!' whispered the Vizier.

'That is his hideous son, who wished to marry me,' said the Owl.

There was a sudden burst of laughter from within the hall, and a voice shouted: 'Tell us what was this word you gave the Caliph which would turn him back to human form?'

'A Latin word,' said Kaschnur. 'Of which language he and his Grand Vizier know nothing. The word was, "Mutabor".'

Without a sound, the two storks hurried back up the dark passage on their long legs, and the Owl floated after them on her white wings. When they reached the open air once more, the Caliph turned, and, throwing caution to the winds, cried, 'Dear Owl, but for your help we should remain storks to the end of our days. We can never thank you enough. I beg you, will you marry me?'

But before she could reply, both he and the Grand Vizier bowed three times to the west, crying, 'Mutabor! Mutabor! Mutabor!' And in the twinkling of an eye they stood once more in their human form.

And the Owl? She had changed into the most beautiful girl you could wish to see.

And so the Caliph and the Princess and the Grand Vizier returned to Baghdad, where the people rejoiced to see them, for Mirza had already begun to oppress them cruelly.

And Kaschnur and his wicked son? The Caliph sent an army to surround the ruin, and both were taken prisoner while they slept off the effects of their feasting and drinking.

And when both had been compelled to sniff the green powder and turn themselves into rats, they ended their days in the ruined chamber in which they had left the Owl, where they could do no further mischief.

And the Caliph and his bride, and, it is to be hoped, the people of Baghdad, all lived happily ever after.

(From Iraq)

The Golden Goose

Once upon a time, there was a poor widow who had three sons. The eldest was so clever that he could read all his books backwards; the second son had a handsome face, and glossy curling moustaches; but the third son had a snub nose, and a wide mouth, and so few brains that everyone called him 'Dummling'.

One cold day, the widow called her eldest son. He came at once, reading his book backwards.

'My clever Nico!' she said. 'I am sorry to disturb your studies, but can you help your poor old mother? The fire has gone out, and the woodshed is empty, and how to cook our supper, this cold day, I am at my wits' end to know.'

'Well now, fuel for the fire?' said Nico, frowning at the fireplace over his spectacles. 'Let me see: there is coal, peat, and wood, etc. etc. But perhaps wood is the most easily found. Yes: wood. Is there not a forest a few miles away?'

'My clever son!' said his mother. 'I knew you would think of something.'

'My dear mother, such a problem is easily solved by a learned man,' said Nico.

So his mother gave him a pasty, baked with the last of the fire, in case he got hungry; and a flask of wine, in case he felt thirsty; and he set off for the forest – but not until the widow had called him back, for he had quite forgotten to take the axe.

On he went, tripping and stumbling, for he was still reading his book backwards as he went. Presently, he felt hungry, so he sat down to eat his pasty and drink his wine. But just when his mouth was quite full, a little old man hobbled up to him.

'Could you spare a bite of food for a poor old fellow?' he asked humbly.

'Food?' said Nico. 'I'm busy: can't you see I am reading – backwards?' he added. 'Don't interrupt! Get along! I've nothing to give to the likes of you!'

'I can see that you are a very clever young gentleman,' said the old man. 'Would I be right in thinking that you are going to cut down a tree with that sharp axe? If you will take my advice, you will start with the little elder tree over there.'

'I assure you, I need no one's advice! I shall cut down that little oak tree. To a man of wisdom and learning, such a simple task is a mere nothing at all.' And, with a great many long words, Nico explained just how he would set about it. But when he came to do it, it was quite another matter. At the first stroke, the axe slipped, and cut his foot. So, crying like a great baby, he ran home to tell his mother.

Next it was the turn of the second son, Ferdinand, to take the axe to the forest. He didn't want to go at all, in case his moustaches came out of curl, or his nose freckled; for he was very vain. When he sat down to eat his chunk of white bread and cheese, who should come up and ask him for some food but the little old man?

'Give you my bread?' said Ferdinand. 'Not me! I need every crumb, to build up my strength to cut down that little beech tree.'

'Of course, of course,' said the little old man. 'How foolish of me to ask. But if I were a handsome young man, with a moustache that curls so splendidly, I should get out of this forest as soon as possible. There are such damp mists after sunset that the tightest curls will go as limp as seaweed.'

'Mists? I might have known it,' said Ferdinand anxiously. 'I must cut my wood and be off.'

So he put on a pair of gloves, in case his hands should blister, and seized the axe. But he got on no better than his brother. At the second stroke, the axe slipped, and cut his finger. So, crying like a great baby, he ran home to tell his mother.

Next it was Dummling's turn. Now, when the little old man came, and asked him for a drink of water and a bite of the stale crust he was eating, Dummling willingly gave him all he had.

'Thank you, young sir,' said the old man. 'One good turn deserves another. If you will take my advice, you will cut down that little elder tree.'

So Dummling took his axe, and with three strokes, down came the tree, and what should fly out of it, with a whirr of wings, but a real live goose? But what a wonderful goose, for it was made of pure gold!

It flew in a circle, three times round, and then,

with a gobble of its golden beak, it landed at Dummling's feet. So home he went in triumph, with the Golden Goose under his arm.

You can imagine how pleased his mother was. 'We can pull out the goose's golden feathers, and sell them to a merchant in the city, and then we shall be rich!' she cried. But at this, I don't know who was most indignant, Dummling or the Golden Goose, which hissed and gobbled angrily. 'The Golden Goose is mine!' said Dummling, 'and I have made up my mind to take her to the palace, and give her to the Princess.'

As he spoke, he picked up the goose. At this, the widow made a grab at the shining bird, so that she could keep at least one golden feather. But imagine her surprise, when she found she couldn't take her hand away! It was stuck fast!

'Nico! Help! Help!' she cried. 'I'm stuck to the Golden Goose!'

And so she was. Nico came running up, but as soon as he tried to pull her away, *his* hand stuck to her apron strings, and he could not stir.

'Ferdinand! Ferdinand! Help! Help!' shouted Nico. 'I'm stuck to mother's apron strings!'

But as soon as Ferdinand tried to pull Nico away, he stuck fast to his brother! Dummling didn't care. 'I'm *still* going to give my Golden

Goose to the Princess, so you will just have to come to the palace too,' he said.

So off they went, like a string of sausages, one behind the other, till presently they met a milk-maid.

'Ferdinand! Ferdinand! Wherever are you going?' she called, and put her hand on his arm to hold him back – and then she stuck fast too.

Next they met the priest, and he stuck to the milkmaid. And when they tried to walk past the sentry at the palace gates, without by your leave or with your leave, he seized the priest, and he stuck fast too!

As he was dragged along, he shouted to Dummling: 'Hi! Come back! Don't you know that the Princess is ill? She hasn't laughed for months, and anyone who makes her laugh will win her hand in marriage!'

Just at that very moment, who should come along but the Princess herself, looking very pale

and sad. But when she saw Dummling, the Golden Goose, the widow, Nico, Ferdinand, the milkmaid, the priest and the sentry, all in a row, like a string of sausages, first she smiled, and then she began to laugh. She laughed so much, that she had to sit down on the marble steps and hold her sides. And everyone in the palace laughed with her, because they were so glad their young mistress was cured.

And that is how Dummling came to marry the Princess, and became a Prince, and his widowed mother never wanted for firewood again.

(*From Germany*)

Bat Soup

When the sun sets, and the evening becomes grey and shadowy, have you ever seen a bat, skittering about the darkening sky, like a piece of burnt paper on a gusty day? There is an African story which says it was not always like this.

Once upon a time, the Bat flew about in broad daylight, just as the birds do, and settled himself down to sleep at night on a branch of a tree.

Now, the Ground Rat admired the Bat more than any other creature, and was proud to call him his best friend. When he was talking to the other animals Rat would say: 'My great friend Bat says . . .' or, 'My great friend Bat thinks . . .' He would follow Bat all day long when he was able, calling to the other creatures: 'See how graceful Bat is when he flies!' or, 'How clever Bat is to hang upside down when he sleeps!'

At first, Bat was pleased at all this praise. He would look with pride at his umbrella-like wings, and say with mock modesty: 'So simple to fly gracefully when you know how.'

After a while the other animals began to make

fun of this. They would nudge one another when Bat fluttered by, and before Rat could speak up they would shout in chorus: 'How graceful Bat is when he flies!' or, 'It is easy to fly gracefully when you know how!' And then they would grin and titter behind their paws.

Bat did nor care for this, and considered it was all the fault of Rat, so that he began to wish his friend was the other side of the world. But say what he would, Rat still went on tagging along behind, saying the same sort of things, which made the other animals laugh more and more.

Since they were first friends, Bat and Rat had taken it in turns to collect herbs and roots and berries to make their evening soup, which they would eat together. Every day when it was the turn of Bat to be the cook, at the first sip Rat would roll his eyes and say: 'Delicious! Why is it that *your* soup is always so much more tasty than *mine*?' Even if Bat had forgotten the salt or let his soup burn or boil over, Rat would exclaim: 'What a wonderful cook Bat is!'

'What a wonderful cook Bat is!' chorused the other animals, and laughed out loud.

At last Bat could bear it no longer, and a wicked plan came into his head. One day he said: 'You think that *your* soup is not as good as *mine*?'

'I should not dare to compare my tasteless stuff with yours,' Rat replied.

'Then tomorrow evening I will show you how I make Bat soup,' said his friend.

Rat was delighted. He ate nothing all day beforehand, so that his inside would have plenty of room for the delicious supper he was expecting.

In the meantime, Bat found two cooking pots, one for himself and one for Rat, and shortly before evening he put one pot on the fire till it boiled and bubbled. Then he took it off the fire and put it beside the other pot which was filled with cold water.

When he had done this he called: 'Rat! Rat! Where are you? It is time for supper! Have you forgotten that tonight I am going to teach you how to make Bat soup?'

'As if I could forget such a thing!' said Rat, when he came scuttling up, all breathless with hurry.

'Then watch what I do,' said Bat. 'And when I have done, you must do exactly the same in your cooking pot, to show that you understand. I have already filled both pots with water.'

'What a noble friend Bat is!' said Rat.

'Now watch closely,' said Bat. 'First, I put my cooking pot on the fire to heat the water.' And as he spoke he placed the pot full of cold water on the fire. 'Then, I take a few leaves of this, and a couple of roots of that, and half a dozen berries growing on the bush behind you, and drop them one after the other in the cooking pot.'

'One after the other in the cooking pot,' repeated Rat earnestly. 'But that is what I always do,' he went on, 'and *still* my soup is not as good as yours.'

'Aha!' said Bat. 'Now I will tell you the real secret of Bat soup, which I would do to no one else but my friend Rat. Come close, and I will whisper it so that no one else shall hear.'

Rat crept close to Bat, who whispered hoarsely in his ear: 'The minute I have dropped the berries in the water, I close my eyes and jump into the pot myself, like this!' And as he spoke, he closed his eyes and jumped into the pot with a great Splash! And the water, which was just comfortably warm, came right up to his chin. 'And there I sit while I count up to ten, so that the soup takes on the delicious flavour of ME!'

Bat sat grinning at Rat while he counted ten, rather quickly, because though the water was merely warm, the bottom of the pot was growing uncomfortably hot. Then he jumped out again, and shook himself dry, so that the flying drops made the fire sizzle again.

'Well, who would have thought it?' said the astonished Rat. 'I could never have invented that if I tried for a hundred years.' Then he added uncertainly: 'But are you sure that *my* ME will taste as nice as *your* ME, when I sit in the soup?'

'That we can only find out by trying,' said Bat,

as he took the cooking pot full of lukewarm water off the fire, and replaced it with the second pot whose water had only recently gone off the boil. 'Now, there is your soup pot. Show me if you remember what I did.'

'How could I ever forget?' said Rat. 'First I take a handful of leaves of this . . .' And he trotted off to pick them. And by the time he came back the water in the cooking pot had just begun to stir.

'Next I get a couple of roots of that . . .' he went on, and while he scrabbled for the roots the water in the pot sent up a wisp of steam.

'Lastly, a handful of berries . . .'

'Those are not ripe enough,' said Bat sharply, for the water was not quite boiling. And while

Rat went back to the bush and picked some riper berries, Bat fanned the fire with his wings, and the water in the pot began to bubble and boil.

'Make haste!' called Bat impatiently.

'And lastly I drop everything in the water one after the other,' panted Rat, as he came running up. 'And I close my eyes, and jump in the pot myself and count ten!' And because Rat's eyes were tight shut he did not see that the water was bubbling and boiling. He dropped in the herbs, and he jumped into the pot – but he did not count ten. All he said was, 'WHEE! . . .Whee! . . . whee!' as the boiling water closed over him.

And that was the end of poor Rat.

But that is not all. The other animals were so angry with Bat for his cruel treatment of Rat that they chased him here and chased him there, every day, for so long, that at last he hardly dared to show himself. He spent all the daylight hours hiding in caves and dark places where he could not be seen. He only came out when it was growing dark, and even then he flittered here and there, never flying in a straight line, so that his enemies should find it almost impossible to catch him.

And that is how he spent the rest of his life, and all bats that came after him.

(From Africa)

The Golden Apples

Long long ago, far away in the cold north, where ice and snow and bitter storms possess the land for nearly all the year round, the men of the north believed that the great god Odin had planted a huge tree. Its roots were deep in the coldest cold of all; its trunk supported Midgard, which was the world of men; and its towering branches held up Asgard, the land of the gods, whose bitter enemies were the Giants, great beings who were wholly wicked. One of the Giants, called Loki, turned from his wicked ways, it was said, and vowed allegiance to Odin. Only in the tricks he played did he show that he was still not made quite as the other gods, who laughed at his odd ways.

One day, Odin was walking in Midgard with his brother Honier, and Loki. For he often went in disguise to the land of men, to help and advise them. As the shadows grew long at evening, they found themselves in a wild mountainous place, where the only sign of life was a few cattle, grazing on the poor grass.

'We have travelled a long way,' said Odin, 'and we are all three hungry.' And he commanded Loki to kill and roast one of the bullocks.

So Loki killed one of the bullocks; and at the foot of a tall rock, so that they should be sheltered from the wind, he made a spit, and set the meat upon it, and underneath he made a fire. Soon the flames were leaping high, and presently the air was filled with the sizzle and smell of roasting meat.

At last Odin said: 'Surely it is cooked now? Let us eat.'

But what was their surprise when they discovered that the chunks of meat on the spit were as raw inside as if the heat of the fire had never touched them.

'If this is one of your tricks, Loki,' said Odin, 'I warn you, a hungry God is not easily amused. Stoke up the fire again.'

So Loki, who this time was quite innocent of any trick, stoked up the fire till the flames leapt and the embers glowed once more.

'Surely it must be cooked by now?' said Honier presently. 'My stomach cries out for food!'

Loki cut into the meat again, but still it was as raw as when it had first been speared on the spit.

'Again! Again!' said Odin. 'Stoke the fire yet again!' But when the meat was cut for the third time it was still as raw as it had been in the beginning.

'There is some enchantment here,' said Odin. As they looked at the bleeding meat, they heard a hoarse, cackling laugh, and there, perched on the rock above them, was a huge Eagle.

'It is my doing that your fire gives out no heat, and your meat is still raw,' said the Eagle. 'I will see that it cooks if you will give me my share when it is done.'

Odin bowed his head in assent, and the Eagle spread his wide wings and flew down from the rock. Then he croaked strangely over the fire, and fanned it with his wings, till the embers glowed even more brightly than before. But as soon as the meat was cooked, he seized the largest chunks in his beak.

'Stop! You greedy cheating creature!' cried Loki. 'That is more than your share!' And, grabbing a large stick, he gave the bird a lusty clout with the end of it, just as he was about to make off with the meat. With a squawk of anger, the Eagle rose from the ground, but, to Loki's surprise, the stick stuck to his feathers where it had struck him, and his hands stuck to the other end of the stick, so that as the great bird rose in the air, Loki was carried up with it.

Now the Eagle flew fast, but only a few feet from the ground, so that Loki's dangling legs

were banged and bruised and scratched by the
rocks and trees and brambles over which he was
dragged.

'Mercy! Mercy!' cried Loki. 'Put me down, or
I shall be dashed to pieces!'

The Eagle opened its curved beak, and the
chunks of meat fell unheeded to the ground. 'I
will release you, but only if you swear to do what
I demand,' he said.

'Who are you, and what is it you demand?'
asked the unhappy Loki.

'I am Thiazi, the Giant of the Winter, in my eagle's disguise, in which I bring the storms and tempests to the world of men. I will put you down only if you swear to bring me from Asgard the Golden Apples of Youth.'

'But that is not in my power!' said Loki. 'The apples are in the charge of the lovely Lady Iduna, who guards them day and night, so that the Gods alone shall eat of them.'

'I do not care a feather for Iduna!' screeched the Eagle. 'I must have the Apples of Youth.'

'But if I steal them, and the Gods cannot eat of them each day, they will become old and grey, and their strength will depart,' said Loki.

'And *I* shall be young and strong for ever in their place!' cried Thiazi triumphantly. 'I shall make frosts so cold that no man can withstand them, my storms shall shake the foundations of Midgard, and no tottering ancient god shall stay me!'

As he spoke, he dragged the wretched Loki over the knife-edged ridge of a high mountain.

'Only put me down, and I swear to do what you ask!' cried Loki.

'So be it,' said Thiazi. 'Before the sun rises seven times on the kingdom of men, you will bring me the Golden Apples of Youth, or I shall take revenge, compared to which your present pain is but the brushing of a feather.'

141

'I swear to do as you wish!' cried Loki. As he spoke, his hands came away from the stick, and he fell to the ground like a ripe fruit.

Bruised and bleeding, he stumbled back to Asgard. He said nothing to anyone of the promise he had made to Thiazi. But how was he to carry out this promise? He could not bring Thiazi to Iduna, for no Giant might set foot in Asgard. Somehow he must think of a way to persuade Iduna to come with him to Midgard, where Giants could walk, unseen by man.

He thought and thought, but it was not till the sun rose on the world of men for the sixth time that he was able to devise a plan. He sought out the Lady Iduna when she was walking in the flowery meadows of Asgard, clasping in her arms the jewelled casket in which were the Golden Apples of Youth.

'Most beautiful lady,' said Loki. 'Tell me, are there such apples as yours growing anywhere else, or are they only to be found in Asgard? Because, as I was walking in Midgard the other day, at the edge of a forest I saw a tree laden with golden fruit that looked just the same as the apples in your jewelled casket.'

'That must never be,' said Iduna in alarm. 'The Golden Apples of Youth are mine and only mine to guard. Show me this apple tree, so that I may judge for myself.'

So Loki took Iduna by the hand, and led her to the rainbow bridge which leads from Asgard to the land of men, and they came to a forest. Iduna was so occupied looking for the apple tree that she did not notice Thiazi, in the shape of an eagle, lurking in the shadows behind them.

Presently they came to the edge of the forest, and there was an apple tree with its branches bowed down with ripe fruit. Iduna looked at them for a moment, and then she laughed. 'These are very fine apples, but they are the palest yellow! They are nothing like my Golden Apples. Is this another of your tricks, Loki?'

But as she spoke, Thiazi, in his eagle form, swooped down, and with a screech of triumph pounced on Iduna, and carried her off, still clasping her precious casket of apples, to his great cold castle of Thrymheim, in the land of the Giants.

It was not long before the Gods missed Iduna, but no one could tell where she had gone. Presently, without the Golden Apples of Youth, they began to grow old and wrinkled and grey, and the strength to wither from their limbs.

At last, Odin called a council of the Gods, and after much talk in their cracked old voices, they sent all the birds of the air to search for the Lady Iduna. When they had flown away, a single raven came and perched on the arm of Odin's throne.

'Why are you too not searching for the Lady Iduna as I commanded?' said Odin sternly.

'Because some days ago I saw the Lady Iduna with Loki, crossing the rainbow bridge that leads to Midgard,' croaked the raven. 'It is he who can tell you where she has gone, and what has happened to her.'

At this, Odin sent for Loki, and after many threats of dire punishment at last he confessed all that had happened, and how Iduna had been carried off to Thiazi's castle in the land of the Giants.

Odin listened in stern silence. 'There is only one way in which you may be forgiven for your treachery,' he said at last. 'And that is by rescuing the Lady Iduna yourself.'

Then Loki said: 'I will save her from Thiazi if the Lady Freya will lend me her magic cloak, so that I may turn myself into what I choose.'

The Lady Freya gladly lent Loki her cloak, and disguised as a falcon, Loki flew away to the icy home of the Giant of the Winter. When he reached the Giant's castle, he saw the Lady Iduna gazing sadly from the narrow window of a tiny turret room where she had been imprisoned, because she would not give up the casket with the Apples of Youth. Still she cradled the casket in her arms, both day and night.

Loki, in his shape of a falcon, flew through the

window, and at once became himself again. 'Where is the Giant Thiazi?' he asked.

'He has gone fishing,' said Iduna.

'Then we have no time to lose,' replied Loki. 'Take this feather from my falcon's wing and wish to be a sparrow, and as a falcon I will carry you back to Asgard.'

'How do I know that this is not another of your evil tricks?' said Iduna. 'It is through your deceit that I am in this terrible place.'

'I deceived you then indeed,' said Loki. 'But it was the only way to save my life. I am here now to save yours. I beg you, do as I bid you.'

So Iduna wished herself a sparrow, and Loki seized her in his falcon's beak and flew through the window towards Asgard.

They had not flown far, before the Giant Thiazi returned from his fishing and found Iduna and the Golden Apples were gone. He looked through the turret window, and saw a falcon in the distance flying away with something in its claws. At once, in his eagle shape, he gave chase.

Now, a falcon in flight is no match for an eagle, and though the falcon beat the air with all his might, Thiazi steadily gained on him. But the falcon flew desperately on. When the gleaming towers of Asgard at last came in sight, it gave him fresh courage, even though now he could hear the beat of the eagle's wings behind him.

From the battlements the Gods had seen their coming. Hurriedly they made a great pile of straw and sticks in their path below them. Just as the falcon had flown over it, in a last despairing effort, the Gods set fire to the straw, which blazed up in a pillar of flame, setting fire to the eagle's wings, and with a hoarse cry he fell spinning into the heart of the fire, and so died.

Then the Gods welcomed Iduna with shouts of joy, and Odin forgave Loki for his treachery. And when the Gods had eaten once more of the Golden Apples, they became young and handsome and strong, and in all Asgard there was great rejoicing.

(*A Norse legend*)

The Seven Ravens

Once upon a time, there lived in Poland, in the middle of a forest, a poor widow, whose husband had been a wood-cutter. She found life hard without him, for she had a daughter, called Masha, and seven sons. It is small wonder that she sometimes grew tired and cross, for she worked all day to keep them fed and clothed.

One evening, when her work in the little house was finished, she went into the forest and picked a basinful of blackberries. 'They are not very many,' she said to herself. 'But made into a pie perhaps there will be enough.'

As soon as her mother reached home, Masha ran to fetch the pie-dish and the flour and the rolling-pin, but the seven sons just shouted, 'Blackberry pie!' And all the time she was heating the oven, and mixing the pastry, and rolling it out and crimping the edges, they were running in and out to see how the pie was getting on. 'Blackberry pie!' they shouted. 'How long will it take to bake? Are the berries sour? Can we have a

147

second helping?' and a hundred other questions, till the poor woman was quite giddy with the noise, and their running round the table.

'For mercy's sake, be quiet, can't you?' she cried at last. 'Just look at the mud you have trampled all over the floor I scrubbed only this morning! Get away with you, out of my sight! I wish you were seven ravens, I do, instead of seven lumping boys with muddy feet!'

The woman was startled to hear a low cackling laugh outside the cottage door, and to her horror, before her eyes, the seven boys dwindled and shrank. Their arms turned to black feathery wings, and their grinning mouths to sharp

pointed beaks, and as seven coal-black ravens, with seven sad croaks, they rose from the floor with a flapping of wings and flew away through the window.

'Stop! Stop! Come back!' called the poor woman. 'I didn't really mean it!'

But the seven ravens were already high above the trees, flying towards the setting sun. Once again there was the same cackling laugh, this time above her head, and a dark flapping shape flew after the disappearing birds.

The unhappy mother was horrified at what she had done. 'Whose was that cackling laugh?' she cried, 'and what was that black shape which flew after my poor boys?' She sat down with her head in her hands, and nothing Masha could say would comfort her. Not even the smell of burning blackberry-pie roused her from her sorrow.

'Perhaps they will come back if we are patient,' said Masha.

But months and years went by, and still they did not come back.

At last Masha said to her mother, 'How sad and dull it is without my brothers! I have made up my mind to search the whole wide world until I find them.'

'The world is a wide wicked place,' said her mother. 'How will you manage to live?'

'I shall take my needle and thread and my little

149

pair of scissors,' said Masha, 'and perhaps I can persuade people to give me supper and a bed in return for some sewing.'

So she said good-bye to her mother and set out to find her brothers. At every house she stopped to sew, she asked if anyone had seen the seven ravens, but everyone just laughed. How should they know her seven ravens among so many in the world?

One day Masha stopped at a grand house with more shining windows than she could possibly count. There she was given a silk shirt to mend. 'It is the young Duke's favourite shirt,' said the servant who handed it to her, 'so your neatest sewing, mind.'

Masha set to work and mended the shirt, and next morning, when the Duke called for it, the servant said, 'A young woman who came to the door asking for work, has mended it so neatly that you need a magnifying glass to see the stitches!'

The Duke turned the shirt this way and that, trying to find the darn. 'Send her to me, so that I may thank her,' he said. But Masha had risen with the sun and was already on her way once more, in search of her seven brothers.

After many weeks of wandering, tired and downhearted she came one day to a clearing in a dense forest. It was a dark and lonely place, which would have scared most people away, but trees had been her friends since she was a little child, so Masha walked cheerfully on. She had walked a long way, when she came to a clearing among the trees, and there before her was the strangest little house she had ever seen. It was as round as the full moon, and seemed to be made of gleaming silver. The tree that grew beside it was covered with silver leaves, which tinkled like a harp with every little breeze.

'This is a strange house!' said Masha to herself. 'But perhaps the people who live in it will give me shelter for the night. I am so tired that I can't walk any further.'

The woman who opened the door was dressed in silver from head to foot. She looked at Masha with surprise, and said crossly, 'Go away! I'm busy. I have no time to talk to strangers. I have the supper to cook, and a great tear in my husband's cloak to mend before he comes home.'

'Won't you let me mend the cloak?' said Masha. 'Then you can get on with cooking the supper.' And she took out her needle and thread and her little pair of scissors.

'Come in then! Come in!' said the woman, who was now all smiles.

Everything in the house seemed to be made of silver. Even the cloak the woman handed her was woven of silver thread.

Masha looked at the great rent, sat herself down on a silver three-legged stool and set to work. She had just finished the last stitch when the door opened, and a man came in. He too was dressed in silver, from the heels of his boots to the feather in his cap.

'I suppose supper is late as usual, wife, and my cloak not mended? How am I to reach the moon tonight without it?' he grumbled.

'You are wrong, husband,' said the woman. 'The chicken is roasted to a turn. And, thanks to this girl you see sitting in the corner, your cloak is mended!'

'Why, so it is!' said the man, taking the cloak from Masha. 'And with stitches so small you need a magnifying glass to see them! If supper is ready, let her sit down and join us.'

Over a delicious supper, the silver man and woman asked Masha who she was, and where she was going. She told them of her long search for her seven brothers.

When they had finished eating, the man said, 'You have helped us, and perhaps I can now repay by helping you. We are Moon People, who visit the earth from time to time, as we do the other planets. Tonight the Moon is full, and there is very little she does not see on earth. I will ask her to look for your seven brothers. Stay here till morning, when I shall return.'

He threw the silver cloak over his shoulders as he spoke. Masha thanked him gratefully, and rose to clear the supper things. She was just about to throw away the chicken bones from the silver dish when the Moon Man said, 'Throw nothing away that may be useful. Put those bones in your pocket.'

Obediently, Masha did as she was told, though she could not think what use a few chicken bones could be.

Then the man went out into the clearing, where he seized the corners of his cloak and stretched out his arms, and at once the cloak became a pair of great shining silver wings, on which he rose from the ground, and flew up and up into the sky, till he was nothing but a silver speck in the light of the setting sun.

When the Moon Man returned at sunrise next day he said, 'I have news which may help you. Many miles from here there is a mountain made of amber. The Moon herself has said that she has seen seven ravens circling round the top, and croaking sadly.'

'My brothers!' cried Masha. 'I am sure they must be! But where is this Amber Mountain, and how can I get there?'

'Follow your nose, and ask,' said the Moon Man. And he stood at the door of the silver house, with the Moon Woman beside him, and waved good-bye to her as she set out once more.

Masha followed her nose for miles and miles, and asked the way to the Amber Mountain from everyone she met, but when, after many days, she reached its great glowing sides, she cried, 'How in the world can I climb a mountain so steep and so slippery? There does not seem to be a foothold for anything bigger than a mouse; nothing but a few cracks and crevices!' And she sat down and burst into tears. But as she sat down, something sharp stuck into her leg. It was one of the chicken bones she had put in her pocket.

'The Moon Man said they might be useful, and I believe they are the very thing I need,' she said to herself. Taking a leg bone, she pushed one end of it into one of the cracks, so that the other end stuck out far enough for her to stand on. Then she took the second leg bone, and pushed it into another crack which was a little higher, and climbed on that. Then, very carefully, standing on the second chicken bone, she pulled out the first, and wedged it into a third crack higher up. In this way she climbed up and up the Amber Mountain. Slowly and painfully at last she reached the top, where she threw herself down on the hard amber surface to get her breath back.

Almost at once, she was roused by a sound she could not mistake. It was the croak of a raven; then another croak, and another. She lifted her head, and at first she could see nothing, for the amber was as smooth and bare as an egg. Then she realised that she was a few feet away from a great pit. Crawling forward, she peered down its glowing golden sides, and there were seven ravens flying round and round below her.

'Brothers! Brothers! It is I, your sister Masha, come to take you home!' she cried. Excitedly the ravens cawed back, but a loud cackling laugh interrupted.

'Not so fast, my pretty dear!' said a harsh grating voice. 'The ravens belong to me! I am the Witch of the Amber Mountain, and I heard your mother wish they were seven ravens instead of seven lumping boys, so I granted her wish, and ravens they became. As ravens they are my slaves, to do my will. There is only one way in which the spell may be broken.'

'Whatever it is, I will do it!' cried Masha.

'For seven years you must be silent,' said the Witch. 'A year for each brother. In that time, you must not speak one single word. On the last day of the seventh year, the spell will be broken.'

'Then I will be silent. Have no fear, my brothers!' cried Masha.

To the sound of the sad croaking of the ravens, mixed with the cackling laugh of the Witch, she began to climb down the mountain the way she had come.

When at last she reached home again, you can imagine how delighted her mother was to welcome her. But, of course, she could tell nothing of her adventures. All she could do was to make signs, to explain that she was unable to speak.

And so Masha settled down to help her mother in silence until the seven years were up.

Four years passed, and she was picking up sticks for the fire one day in the forest, when a party of horsemen burst through the bushes.

Masha was so startled that she dropped the sticks.

'Do not be alarmed, my dear,' said the foremost rider and dismounting from his horse, he helped her to pick them up again.

'My Lord Duke,' said one of his companions, 'I do believe this is the same young woman who mended your shirt so neatly. I could not mistake that pretty face!'

The Duke was so pleased with Masha that he seemed to find an excuse to ride by the widow's house each day after that. At last he asked her to marry him. With nods and smiles and a deep curtsey, Masha consented.

And so she went to live in the grand house with more shining windows than she could count. And very happy the young couple were. Her husband did not seem to mind that she could not speak, and their happiness was complete when she had a bonny little baby boy.

Now the Duke had a sister, who was jealous of Masha, and ashamed that her brother should have married a common peasant girl, and one who could not speak into the bargain. One evening, when her brother returned from a visit which had lasted several days, she said to him, 'You will be sad to see that your little son has been taken ill, and sadder still to hear the cause. Your wicked wife has been dropping poison in his food, because she thinks you love your son more than you love your wife. She does not know I have seen her at her evil tricks.'

The Duke was shocked when he saw his little son, lying pale and still and near to death in his cradle. (Masha, of course, could not explain, but she knew it was a plot of the wicked sister's, for it was she who had dropped poison in the baby's food. She had caught her in the very act, and had knocked the spoon and poison bottle from the wicked woman's hand.)

'If this is true, you are not fit to be alive!' said the Duke to Masha. 'You are too dangerous to go free. You shall have seven days in which to repent of your wickedness: on the seventh, you will be executed. Until then you will be locked in the Prison Tower.'

For six long days Masha remained a prisoner in the Tower. On the morning of the seventh day when she was to die, the gaoler, who was sorry for his young captive, brought her a few cherries. When she had eaten them, she sat counting the stones on her plate. 'One, two, three, four, five, six, seven . . .' she counted. And as she said 'Seven', outside the Tower she heard the croaking of ravens.

She ran to the window. She could see seven black birds wheeling round in the morning sky. 'Seven cherry stones, seven ravens, seven years!' she said to herself. 'I believe the time is up!'

She opened the narrow window, and one by one the seven ravens flew in, and as each one landed on the bare floor it turned, in the twinkling of an eye, into one of her seven brothers!

What rejoicing and laughter there was! The seven brothers, now grown into handsome young men, told the astonished Duke their story, and how Masha's courage had rescued them from the Witch of the Amber Mountain. And then Masha told her own story, and her husband was ashamed that he had ever suspected her, and begged her forgiveness. It was now the jealous sister's turn to be shut up in the Prison Tower. The little baby recovered his rosy cheeks and happy smiles, and they all three lived happily ever after.

And the seven brothers? They went home to the cottage in the forest, and their mother wept with joy to see them. She never scolded them again – at least, not often, and then she was very careful what she said!

(From Poland)

Postscript

There was once a Holy Man who lived in Ireland. It was said that he had no possessions; nothing in the world. But he had three companions: a cock, a mouse and a fly, who helped him with his worship.

How in the world did they do this, you ask? I will tell you.

The cock crowed to wake him in time to say the first prayers of the day.

The mouse nibbled his ear if he fell asleep again, for he nodded off easily, as old men will.

And the fly?

As his friend studied the holy books, the good little creature would keep pace with him by running along above each line; and if the old man was called away from his reading, it would sit, quite still, on the very word at which he had stopped, so that he should not lose his place.

(From Ireland)